HEARTBEAT

Books in
The Jennifer Grey Mystery Series

HEARTBEAT

*A
Jennifer Grey
Mystery*

Jerry B. Jenkins

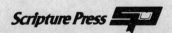

Scripture Press

AMERSHAM-ON-THE-HILL, BUCKS HP6 6JQ
ENGLAND

© 1986 Jerry B. Jenkins

This book was first published in the United States by
Moody Press. Copyright 1986 by Jerry B. Jenkins

Scripture Press Foundation edition printed by permission
of Moody Bible Institute, Chicago, Il.

First British edition 1990

ISBN 1 872059 03 1

Production and Printing in England for
SCRIPTURE PRESS FOUNDATION (UK) LTD
Raans Road, Amersham-on-the-Hill, Bucks HP6 6JQ by
Nuprint Ltd, 30b Station Road, Harpenden, Herts AL5 4SE.

1 At 12:53 a.m., Tuesday, December 6, Jennifer Grey awoke to the sound of the telephone beside her bed. 'I know you don't want me to call you unless it's important, but I think this is hot.' It was the voice of Robert Block, her young assistant at the *Chicago Day*.

'That's all right, Bobby,' she said. 'What've you got?'

'Another big internal bust. Lots of top names from the Sixteenth Precinct, but somebody went down tonight.'

'Someone was shot?'

'Yup, don't know who yet. Rumour is someone from Internal Affairs.'

'Killed?'

'Think so, but nobody's talking.'

'Where are you?'

'The office. Leo told me you'd want to handle this yourself and to just stay by the phone.'

'He's right.'

'I could handle it for you, Jennifer, if you wanted me to, I mean.'

Jennifer smiled at his earnest naïvety. 'I'll call you from the Sixteenth, Bobby. But thanks anyway.'

Jennifer spent less than two minutes washing her face and applying light makeup. She pulled her long, light-brown hair into a ponytail and threw on what she always thought of as her emergency outfit — a white, button-down blouse under a burnt-orange V-neck sweater, a brown plaid, pleated skirt, and zippered boots.

She grabbed her calf-length camel-hair coat and slung over her shoulder a large bag containing the usual essentials plus her reporter's spiral note pad.

She paused near the phone in the living room, wondering if this was the one time she could justify taking advantage of her relationship with Jim. She had enjoyed a lovely dinner with him just hours before at a quiet spot not frequented by newspaper people or policemen.

She knew it was risky, if not wrong, for a police reporter to be seeing a policeman. But she rationalized that if she didn't use him as a source of information and left writing about him to the feature writers — his current assignment took him into primary and secondary schools as Officer Friendly — no one had to know.

Besides, she wasn't sure how she felt about him. It was clear how he felt about her. But a widow of fewer than three years who still thought of her late husband every day was not jumping into any new relationship.

There was no need to bother Jim in the middle of the night. Chiding herself for having even thought of waking him, she sat on the edge of the sofa and dialled the Sixteenth Precinct station instead.

'Yeah, somethin' went down, Sweetheart,' Desk Officer Flannigan told Jennifer. 'But if I tell ya over the phone, that means I won't get to see yer pretty face down here tonight, right?'

'Please, Herb,' she said, 'you can't joke about someone getting killed, can you?'

Silence.

'Herb?'

'Who bought it, Jenny? I didn't know anybody bought it. I heard a guy took a coupla slugs in the gut, but I didn't know he died.'

'Who was it, Herb?'

'Somebody from IAD, but you know I can't tell you anything. You sure he died? I didn't hear he died.'

'My source wasn't sure either, Herb. I just thought you might know.'

'You don't know any more'n I do. What're

you doin' talking about somebody dyin' when you don't know?'

'I'm sorry, all right? Can I talk to Campbell? Is he on tonight?'

'He's on, but he's talkin' to nobody, 'specially the press. And I'm not supposed to either. You understand?'

'If I come down there, can I see him?'

'I doubt it, but then I'd get to see you, so don't let me talk you out of it.'

Jennifer might have appreciated the dubious compliment under other circumstances. But she had been poking around the grimy precinct station houses for almost a year since graduating from obituaries and school board meetings, and she had no inkling of more Internal Affairs Division activity right under her nose. A major operation had taken place with her on the beat every day, yet she knew nothing about it.

Worse still, someone from Internal Affairs was probably fighting for his life. A new widow might be in the making, and she felt that pain again.

She phoned downtown headquarters, but she got no new leads. *Jim will understand*, she decided. But the phone at his apartment just rang and rang.

Shortly after midnight, a task force for the Internal Affairs Division of the Chicago Police Department had scheduled the operation that would rock the department to its core.

Yet another contingent of Chicago's finest had been caught wallowing in its own mire. Not yet a year and a half since the biggest internal scandal in its history had seen dozens of police officers sentenced to prison for trafficking in drugs, another black eye on the police department's reputation was swelling.

No one — least of all the guilty officers — knew of the investigation. Most officials and citizens and even the press assumed that the last housecleaning had scoured the department of the worst offenders and probably scared the small-timers into staying straight.

But a tiny, close-knit unit from IAD had been keeping an eye on suspicious activity in the Sixteenth Precinct for nearly thirty months — in fact, since long before the more publicized crackdown had even been initiated.

This band of four were players in one of the most dangerous games in the world. Not even their families could know of their activities. They had been given routine assignments, many requiring uniforms, while in reality they were undercover agents, spying and ratting on their own colleagues.

There can be no more despised good guy than the one who must make his living deceiving his friends, being a snitch, an informer. It took a special kind of person to even be considered for such an assignment, and only those a cut above the rest lasted a year.

When you were suspected of reporting to Internal Affairs, you were shunned even by your friends, even by good cops who had nothing to hide. You were quietly ridiculed for being a goody-two-shoes, an idealist, a superpatriot, a God-squadder. And soon enough, of course, you had to be reassigned. A known employee of Internal Affairs was worthless.

Thus, the noisy crackdown that resulted in arrests and convictions and sentences for so many Chicago cops made the smallest IAD unit fear for the success of their own surveillance of the Sixteenth Precinct.

Would their activities be revealed in the course of the trial? Would the success of the bigger mission scare off their prey before they could lower the net? No one from the special unit had been involved in the major crackdown, but would all the publicity somehow tip their hands?

Would Jennifer Grey, the woman they begrudgingly admired for always being in the right place at the right time, somehow sniff out this terribly delicate operation? Could she or the *Day* be persuaded that their First Amendment rights should be voluntarily limited for the sake of human lives?

For months after the publicity of the previous noisy crackdown, IAD laid low, finally realizing that their mission had not been aborted. Their targets had become more cautious, but the lure of profit had finally brought them scurrying back into the cesspool.

And the men from IAD, the ones who had avoided suspicion and had been able to rise above the feeling that they were betraying their comrades, if drug-dealing policemen could be considered comrades, were waiting.

They waited for the perfect time. They waited for the perfect opportunity. They waited until they had something solid on each of the three men and one woman they had been tailing.

The midnight roundup was to be a simple manoeuvre. At a meeting earlier in the day, the four IAD officers had mapped careful strategy, plotting the whereabouts of their marks. Lieutenant Frank Akeley would be easy. He'd leave his favourite watering hole on Wells Street at exactly midnight, and IAD Chief John Lucas and two specially assigned patrolmen — who would not know what they were going to be involved in until about half an hour in advance — would make the arrest, booking Akeley downtown in an attempt to avoid publicity as long as possible.

The two others would be trickier. Sergeant Bill Much was a family man and would be asleep at home, if everything went as expected. No one looked forward to the prospect of an arrest in the dead of night, especially when a man's family would suddenly realize what was going on.

They'd think it was a mistake, of course, but Sergeant Much would know. And he could be armed. And there could be trouble. IAD Special Investigator Ray Bequette had the assignment, and he also would take two uniformed police officers with him.

For Officer James Purcell, IAD had decided on a ruse. He was a bachelor, living alone in an apartment on Oak Street near Rush. IAD investigator Donald Reston, a rangy, athletic, youthful man in his late thirties, would call Purcell from the lobby and tell him he had information on one of his cases. Reston would say he was sorry to bother him, but could they come up, and all the rest. When Purcell activated the buzzer and let them in downstairs, they could only hope he would still be unaware of what they were up to.

At least the bust that would end Reston's stint in IAD (anything publicized ruined future effectiveness) would be one the public would love. They turn on their heroes the first chance they get, and Purcell was a bona fide turncoat against the public trust.

Any bad cop was, of course, but this one

would go down the throat of John Q. Public like nectar. A bad cop with a good reputation who gets his comeuppance. For Reston, it was too good to be true.

Officer Trudy Janus would be on duty on the street. Her partner would be directed to phone the station for a personal message. When he stopped to place the call, IAD's Eric O'Neill, a uniformed officer, and a police matron would arrest Janus.

It was set. Warrants had been issued. And not more than eight people in the world knew what would be going down. Fewer than that knew when and who and how. The mayor and the police commissioner knew the basics. IAD Chief Lucas, the three others in the operation, and a secretary knew everything.

Lucas was convinced that his men had not breathed a word to anyone, not anyone. Not a friend, not a relative, not a lover. If ever there was a business in which you couldn't trust *anyone*, this was it. Not that a man like Ray Bequette couldn't trust his wife of twenty years, but who might she tell? What might slip? Who knew what information might get to the wrong ears?

That was one reason that short terms with IAD were the norm. A man couldn't carry the burden of guilt and suspicion long without being able to tell even his own loved ones.

The operation was to be simultaneous,

with the four suspects being brought downtown by 12:30 a.m. Sergeant Bill Much
would be last, as his arrest would take place
on the city's far West Side. Many more
officers and civilians were involved, of
course, but one thing was sure: these four
were the ringleaders, the principal drug
buyers and suppliers. And when they fell,
they'd bring a massive network down with
them.

At 11:00 p.m. IAD Chief John Lucas had
sat in his personal car on the other side of
the street and a half block to the south of the
tiny car-park of The Illusion bar near the
corner of Wells and Ontario. Unmarked
squad cars would never work for Internal
Affairs; they were just as recognizable by
cops as were the standard blue and white
patrols.

Lucas, a tall, thin, greying man in his late
fifties, was as respected as a man in his
position could be. His was a thankless job.
Neither he nor the people above him ever
really liked what he ferreted out. Yet no
one, not even those who had been burned
by his professional approach and his
incredible reputation for confidentiality in a
huge police department, questioned his
motives.

He was always impeccably dressed and
soft-spoken. He shunned publicity. He personally handled the arrests of police officers
above the rank of sergeant, and as difficult

as it must have been for him, he was somehow usually able to pull them off with the
least humiliation for the suspect.

That, he told his superiors more than
once, would come in greater measure than
he could ever personally mete out, when
the man had to face his own family and the
press and the public in court. 'It is not my
job to destroy a man before his subordi-
nates. By the time I get to him, he has
already accomplished that on his own. My
role is to clean the house quickly and
deliver the man to his fate.'

His prey had entered the bar, as usual, a
few minutes after ten-thirty. While Lucas's
men began to close their stakeout nets
around Sergeant Bill Much's West Side
house and Officer James Purcell's Near
North apartment and Trudy Janus's squad
car, Lucas himself unhurriedly left his car
and strode to a phone booth on the corner,
another half block north.

He could still keep an eye on the bar's
side exit — the one Lieutenant Frank Akeley
would use to get to his car. Lucas and his
men had talked about having a squad car
merely pull Akeley over with a story of a
defective rear-light or some other minor
infraction. Then, when his guard was down,
he would be arrested and read his rights.

But Lucas had decided against it. Too
dangerous, he believed. Akeley was usually
able to pilot himself to his apartment,

despite the fact of driving while under the influence. But Lucas didn't know specifically what kind of a drunk Frank Akeley made. He was armed. Would he cry or pass out, or would he reach for his piece? It was too great a risk for the patrolman or two who would have no idea what it was all about until it was over.

Lucas dialled. 'Sixteenth Precinct, Flannigan.'

'Good evening, Officer Flannigan,' Lucas began carefully. 'Chief Lucas calling for the sergeant on duty.'

'Yeah, who's 'is again?'

'Chief Lucas calling.'

'An' you want Sergeant Campbell?'

'If he's the sergeant on duty, yes sir.'

'Is this Lucas from IAD?'

'Yes, sir.'

'What's goin' down? Somethin' big?'

'Flannigan,' Lucas grew cold. 'I need to speak to your watch commander. Will you put him on please?'

Lucas directed Campbell to assign two patrolmen to meet him at the phone booth as soon as possible. 'Oh, please, Chief, you're not gonna bust somebody right here on my shift, are ya?' Campbell pleaded.

'As a matter of fact, no, Sergeant, and you know I can't discuss it further. May I expect a couple of officers?'

'Yes, sir.'

Lucas turned his collar up against the

cold wind and buried his hands deep in the pockets of his long trench coat. When a squad car pulled to the curb, he slipped into the back seat and briefed the officers.

They began by radioing in that they would be unavailable for more than an hour. Lucas told them precisely what he was doing and — not so precisely — why. 'You will station yourself in front of the bar, out of the light,' he told the one, 'and you will be in front of the next building to the north. When I leave my car and cross the street, I will approach Lieutenant Akeley and call him by name, as if in a greeting.

'If he merely looks up in surprise, just fall in behind me in the car-park to back me up. I'll identify myself officially, show him my badge, and ask him to surrender his weapon. If he resists, I'll ask you to assist me. Don't draw your guns unless I ask you to or unless it becomes obviously necessary.'

The officers, one young and the other old, were stony. Neither liked his assignment, but Lucas didn't detect any treason in their silence. He didn't much like his own assignment for that matter. Nonetheless, this wasn't the time for convincing the patrolmen of the lieutenant's guilt. They wouldn't attempt to tip anyone off by radio, because they knew he would be monitoring the frequency in his own car.

'Take your positions at eleven fifty-five, unless you see me leave my car earlier.'

Lucas headed back to his own car and maintained his vigil, shaking his head slightly at the thought of the watch commander worrying that one of his own men might be used by IAD. *What will he think when he finds out it's his boss, the lieutenant who likes to work the three to eleven shift, but always leaves for The Illusion at ten-thirty?*

On the West Side, Ray Bequette had rolled to a stop about a block from Bill Much's home. The only light visible in the house was a flickering television from an upstairs window. Bequette had briefed his assigned officers on the way from downtown. One moved quietly between houses to cover the back door; the other carefully hid in the shrubbery at the front of the small house.

'I'll ring the bell, and we'll just have to see what he does,' the stocky forty-five-year-old veteran whispered. He had aspired to a position with IAD since its inception when he was a young cop. When he secretly supplied information leading to the arrest of not only three men on his shift, but also his own partner, in a shakedown scheme, IAD was able to keep his name out of it and put him on other cases while providing another assignment as the perfect front. He was ostensibly in charge of records and vehicles at the smallest precinct in the city. There was no way to keep his name out of this one. When he personally arrested a sergeant, the word would spread quickly and his undercover days in IAD would end.

At the Oak Street apartment of Officer James Purcell, Donald Reston had worried that Purcell would smell a rat. So when Purcell sounded not the least bit perturbed at being awakened by a phone call from the lobby and quickly agreed to let Reston and two others come up to see him, Reston sent one cop to one end of the landing and the other one to the other end and approached Purcell's door carefully.

Eric O'Neill had arranged for an emergency personal call to be placed to the precinct station for the partner of Officer Trudy Janus. When the dispatcher related the message, 'Ten-twenty-one the station, personal,' Janus's partner stopped at the next call box. As he neared the phone, the uniformed officer approached to tell him what was happening, while O'Neill and the matron closed in on the unsuspecting woman in the squad car.

2 Officer Trudy Janus's partner had been puzzled when he was interrupted before reaching for the call-box phone. 'There's no call,' Eric O'Neill's backup told him. 'IAD just needed you out of the car for a minute.' He wheeled around to see O'Neill flash his badge through the passenger side window of the squad while the matron positioned herself near the rear-light on the other side.

Janus angrily yanked at the door handle, but O'Neill pressed against the door, both palms facing her. 'You can step out,' he said, 'but I want to see those hands.'

'What're you, bustin' me?' she asked.

'You got it. Lemme see those hands.'

'I'm not goin' for the gun,' she said, disgusted and swearing. 'Hey, you can't collar me without a woman here anyway!' O'Neill pointed to the matron. When Janus craned her neck to look, O'Neill opened the door and asked her to unsnap her holster.

'Was my partner in on this setup?' she demanded.

'No.'

'What's this all about?'

'You wanna just come downtown with me and find out, Trudy, or you want me to read you your rights right here while a crowd gathers?'

She stepped from the car and slammed the door.

'Should I have her search you, or you wanna give me your other piece?'

Janus pulled a tiny .22 from her left ankle.

'Is that everything?'

She nodded, glaring.

James Purcell had opened his apartment door to find Donald Reston out of his direct line of sight on the landing with his snub-nosed .38 in his hand. 'Whoa! I'm unarmed, Don,' Purcell said, barefoot in pyjama bottoms and a T-shirt. 'Search me.'

'I'm on a job from IAD,' Reston told him, almost apologetically, and holstered his pistol. He signalled to his backups, and they entered the apartment.

'What's it all about, Don?' Purcell asked.

'It's about drugs,' Reston said. 'Isn't it usually about drugs?'

'Not always,' Purcell said.

Reston squinted at him, wondering what he meant. 'You wanna just come with us, or do you need me to officially arrest you here?'

'Nah. I'll come.' Purcell didn't even appear offended.

When Ray Bequette had rung the front door-bell at the Bill Much residence, a huge figure appeared at the window upstairs. Ray waved, and Much opened the window. 'Who'sat? Bequette? What're you doin' here, Ray?'

'I'm here for IAD, Bill. I'm sorry.'

Much was bending over with both hands on the windowsill, his massive body still. He stared down at Bequette, a man he'd never worked with, but who had been a classmate at recruit school more than twenty years before.

Much's shoulders heaved and he began to sob. 'Do I gotta come with you right now?' he whined.

'Yeah,' Bequette whispered.

'Oh, no.' Still Much didn't move except to draw a hand to his mouth and muffle his whimpering. 'Oh, no, no.' And he swore.

'C'mon down, Bill,' Bequette said. 'Just come on downtown with us, huh?'

'You're not alone?' the big man said.

'I got somebody at the back and somebody here with me,' Ray said, and his front garden man extricated himself self-consciously from the bushes.

'Oh, you didn't have to do that, Ray. You know me. I ain't gonna hurt nobody. I'll come with ya. Just give me a minute.'

'Bill?'

'Yeah.'

'You come without your piece, hear?'

''Course, Ray. I don't wanna hurt nobody.' Lights began to come on in other rooms.

When Sergeant Bill Much, who would never wear a badge again, emerged from his house, he wore bedroom slippers, no socks, work trousers with an elasticated waistband, a sweatshirt, and a short, unbuttoned jacket. He carried a carrier bag with a change of clothes. And no gun.

'Am I gonna be gone long?' he asked Bequette.

'Probably so.'

'My wife can bring my other stuff in the morning,' he said absent-mindedly. He sat in the front seat next to Bequette, carefully placed the bag next to him, pressed his fingers to his forehead, and cried quietly all the way downtown.

When Bequette drove through the underground garage to the lift that would take Much to the interrogation room, he saw Reston's and O'Neill's cars. John Lucas had not arrived yet, so Bequette, as special investigator, had to officially arrest and

charge Much, Purcell, and Janus and see
that they were properly booked.

Janus sat in a straight-backed wooden
chair, coolly answering O'Neill's questions.
She looked up in disgust at Bill Much's red,
puffy eyes. Jim Purcell leaned against a
counter, chatting amiably with a booking
clerk.

He jerked quickly to attention with a
stricken look when the rumour reached the
booking room that 'Lucas is down! They've
taken him to Henrotin Hospital!' Much gri-
maced. Janus suppressed a smile.

John Lucas's backup officers had moved
into position at 11:55 p.m. as instructed, and
Lieutenant Frank Akeley left the bar six
minutes later. He may have been tipsy, but
it didn't show in his walk. He was in plain
clothes, moving briskly between vehicles to
his own car.

Lucas's path intersected Akeley's line of
vision, but the lieutenant apparently
decided not to turn and look, despite the
fact that he had to have seen Lucas
peripherally. 'Frank!' Lucas called, yet still
the man didn't slow or turn.

By continuing, Lucas would have blocked
Akeley, but he hesitated, then stepped forward again, falling in behind Akeley.
'Frank!' he tried again, knowing full well
that even an inebriated man would have
heard him.

Akeley stopped, but he didn't turn around. Lucas signalled for his backups and put his hand on Akeley's shoulder. 'What *do* you want, Lucas?' Akeley shouted, his back still to him.

'You know what I want, Frank. Don't make it difficult for both of us.' He was glad Akeley's hands were in his overcoat pockets and that the coat was buttoned. He couldn't go for his shoulder holster without unbuttoning his coat.

But as Akeley turned around, the hand hidden by his body pulled a .22 from his coat pocket, and he fired three times as he faced Lucas. The IAD chief lurched forward, his face ashen, and he grabbed Akeley's lapels, dragging him to the ground before releasing his grip. Lucas was unconscious, bleeding from two holes in his abdomen and one hole in his chest.

'Police! Freeze!' the uniformed officers screamed as they dropped to crouching positions, each with both hands on service revolvers pointed at Akeley's head.

'Self-defence, self-defence! Lucas tried to kill me!' He still had the weapon in his hand.

'Drop it, or you're dead!'

'I'm your superior!' Akeley said, trying to pull himself up from under Lucas's weight.

'The man never made a move on you, Lieutenant!' the officer said, pulling back the hammer of the .38 with his thumb.

Akeley let the .22 slip from his fingers and slumped again to the pavement as the other cop kicked it away.

'You probably killed the man,' the first said. 'We gotta call an ambulance.'

Jennifer Grey tried to watch her speed as she hurried to the Sixteenth Precinct station house. She remembered the warning of Leo Stanton, her city editor, that he would bail her out of jail for whatever it took for her to get a story — except a traffic offence.

His idea of police reporting and hers were light years apart. But he was the one with thirty-five years in the business who had been on the police beat 'when cops were cops and newspapers were newspapers'.

With Leo Stanton in the slot, the *Chicago Day* would always have an old-fashioned, high quality, complete city news section, 'even if,' he was fond of saying, 'the rest of the rag goes to psycho-babble, pinko columnists, and how to develop a meaningful relationship with your dog'.

She enjoyed working for Leo, even if she couldn't stand the unlit cigar lodged in the corner of his mouth. Occasionally he'd slide it free with two fingers and a thumb and she'd have to endure looking at the soggy end, but he was a bit more articulate when his plug was pulled.

He'd had the crazy thing in the first night when she turned in a story he didn't like.

She was new on the police beat and had written what he called 'a feminine piece'.

'But I'm a woman,' she had tried. 'I'm going to sound more like a woman than a man. I can't change that can I?' He glared at her. 'Should I?'

'You should sound like a newspaper reporter, not a man *or* a woman. People don't want to read *you*. They want to read your story. Write it like a reporter, not like a pretty little lady.'

He shoved her story back across the desk, and she couldn't resist yanking it from his grip. She knew she shouldn't have, but she was fuming, talking to herself. She headed back to her typewriter, but he called her back.

'This time,' he said, 'remember that you're in the city room now, not the society page or wherever in the world we inherited you from. Write it on the tube and patch it over to mine. I'll edit it on the screen.'

It had taken her until midnight to learn the rudiments of the video display terminal so she could rewrite the story. Robert Block, a journalism student from Northwestern University who was to be her assistant, walked her through it and even showed her how to transmit her story to Leo when she was ready.

Twice she had lost everything but her notes, but finally the piece was finished. She sent it electronically to Leo's machine.

When it came up on the screen, he hollered across the city room, 'This better be good; I'm two hours into overtime now, and everybody knows *I* don't get paid overtime.'

She was still furious. *Everybody's seen your salary posted with all the other Guild rates too,* she thought, *and if we made that kind of money, we wouldn't care about overtime.* And as she sat waiting for his reaction, she realized how good it was to feel some real emotion again after so long.

After Scott had been killed in a car crash just before their first anniversary, Jennifer had retreated to her parents' home in Rockford. She wanted to do nothing, to say nothing, to think nothing. When the shock wore off and the pain invaded, she slept twelve to sixteen hours at a stretch and didn't want to eat.

Her parents had been supportive, but her father brought her back to reality with his gentle speculation that her sleep was just a substitute for what she really wanted. She wanted to die, he said. She wanted to join Scott. She knew in an instant that he was right. And that she couldn't. And that the same God she had trusted as a child and had worshipped and prayed to all her life would bring her through this.

She knew it in her head, but that didn't make her feel any better. Though her father's counsel forced her back into a semblance of normal routine, the numbness, the absence of any emotion, hung with her like a colourless cloud even after she had moved away from home again. She found her own apartment and finished her journalism degree. Then she landed a job on the new *Day*, mostly because they wanted an entire staff that had not worked on a Chicago paper before.

She wrote obituaries and then covered board meetings, and her no-nonsense reporting style caught Leo's eye. Whenever he got on to her about anything, she reminded herself that *he* had sought *her* out, not the other way around. He was the one who thought she had the makings of an excellent police reporter. He was the one who said she could go places and that there was no better starting place than the toughest beat in the city.

'You'll be up against the best the *Tribune* and the *Times* have to offer,' he said. 'And they won't give you a thing.'

On that first night, her anger at her new boss made her realize that she was emerging again. After a couple of years in emotional limbo, the temper that had so tried her mother, the temper she had even hidden from her young husband, the temper she had tentatively and unsuccessfully tried to turn on God when He snatched her love away came bubbling up to make her feel alive again.

Everyone knew what it was like to work

for Leo. And everyone wanted to. You'd never learn so much so fast or be pushed to such limits or set such standards for yourself working for anyone else. But that didn't lessen her ire any when he read her rewrite and yelled at her again.

She stood at the rim of his horseshoe desk and heard him say one word she didn't understand. Was it *good? Bad? Better? Worse?*

'I'm sorry?' she said.

He repeated it, only this time it sounded like a foul expletive. It wasn't that she hadn't ever heard the word before; she just wasn't sure she'd heard it this time.

'I didn't hear you,' she said.

He pulled his cigar from his lips, as if to aid his articulation, then thought better of it and waved her back to her desk. When she arrived, her screen was blinking. She called up the message and blinked herself. There on the screen, from her new boss, was the four-letter word she thought she'd heard.

She didn't want Leo to see her redden, more from anger than embarrassment. She tapped out a return message. 'Does that mean you like my story, or you don't?'

'I don't,' came the reply.

'Can you tell me why, or is vulgarity all I get?'

'There's no more time to mess with it. I'll rewrite it.'

'Then you take the byline in the morning paper.'

'The city editor take a byline on the front page? It's your stuff, your work. Anyway, I'm in charge of who gets bylines.'

'It feels ridiculous writing you messages from twenty-five feet away. Just know that I'm going to succeed in this job and make you like me; appreciate me, anyway.'

'*It* doesn't feel ridiculous. *You* do. So do I. And my liking you is of little consequence to the job we're paid to do. Appreciate you? I already do. Now go home, and in the morning, enjoy the story under your name. It'll be good.'

And it had been good. Leo was a pro. The best. Earthy, but a mentor, nonetheless. They had not communicated, except face to face, since that first night. In fact, he had apologized for his language.

'I didn't know you were religious,' he explained.

'I wouldn't call myself religious,' she had said. 'We can talk about it sometime.'

'No, we can't. And I'm glad you don't call yourself religious, because religion doesn't go far on the police beat. You'll see.'

A pro, a good mentor and all, but not always right. Jennifer had seen how the police beat and her faith fitted together or didn't fit all right, and she had to wonder how she would have survived without it.

She prayed now as she parked on the

street across from the Sixteenth Precinct. She prayed for the injured cop, whoever he was. For his wife. For his family. For the people who would be hurt by this latest internal crackdown, whatever it was all about. For the people who had been hurt by unscrupulous cops in the first place, because there were always civilian victims when policemen went bad.

As she trotted across the street and up the steps to face the greasy Flannigan, she prayed for her Jim. He hadn't been pressed into late duty for months. She knew he wasn't scheduled for tonight.

But if the internal affairs arrests were significant or widespread, maybe a lot of the guys in the Sixteenth would be on the street.

3 James Purcell had been one of the first men Jennifer had met in her new role with the *Day*. He'd been a detective in the Vice Control Division who had requested a transfer due to his personal scruples.

Much had been made of it in the papers because scruples hadn't been a problem in the Chicago Police Department for as long as anyone could remember. 'I don't want to come off like a Sunday school type,' the *Sun-Times* had quoted him. 'But there are things a VCD detective has to do that make it hard for me to sleep at night. I want to see vice controlled in Chicago, but it takes a different kind of a man to do this job.'

The public had taken him to its heart. What he really wanted, he said, was an assignment in the Homicide Division. There was a 'Jim Purcell' day and even a fan club. But it all blew over shortly after the police commissioner announced that it was not up to an individual officer to choose his assignment. The commissioner said he and his command officers would decide whether a man could beg to be let off an assignment, and that even if they decided that such requests might be tolerated, there would be no selecting of the new assignment.

The implications were clear. An officer might request a transfer, but it would not have to be honoured, and there was no guarantee he wouldn't be sentenced to some Siberia within the department, like the night desk clerk's job in the Sixteenth Precinct. Which is what Purcell received.

When Jennifer was making the rounds that first week, she found herself coming back again and again to the shy, younger-than-his-years-looking bachelor at the Sixteenth. She hadn't even entertained a thought of interest in him or any man, but she was scrambling in her job and she needed help. Other desk officer types on her beat leered at her. The brass tolerated her but hardly talked to her. Some tested her. Some made passes at her. Many treated her as a child.

She wanted to do a good job. She wasn't there to do public relations work for the police department, but she wasn't out to get anybody either. All she wanted was information. Solid, truthful, no games, complete information she could use to write a story the public had the right to hear.

Jim Purcell seemed to understand that when no one else did. And though he had said he didn't want to be considered a Sunday school type, he *was* a Sunday school type, and the kids he taught on Sunday mornings demanded an explanation after that quote appeared.

He was like an oasis. She could count on a smile from him even when she stopped at the station house in the middle of the night. She knew that at the end of the counter in front of his desk, she'd find a little wire basket full of copies of all the reports of arrests in the precinct since she'd dropped in last.

Her predecessor had told her about the wire baskets that were unpublicized sources of information to the press and the public. No one used them but the police reporters, and they were not to take the sheets or make photocopies. The desk officers in many station houses thought it amusing to 'misplace' all but the stray dog or cat-up-a-tree reports or, worse, drop in bogus reports.

Jim had rescued her from that humiliation as well. She showed up one night, took her usual copious notes based on the reports in the basket, heard once again that the watch commander didn't have time to talk to her about any of them, and proceeded to tell Jim of a report she had read in the last station house.

Jim's eyes grew wide with mock wonder as she recounted the story of a young mother who had reportedly been startled by an intruder. 'But she just took the matters into her own hands. She shushed him with a finger to her lips as she rocked the baby, giving the intruder a look that said he'd better not wake the baby, whatever he did. Then she continued singing lullabies to the baby while the man sat on the floor. Within a few minutes, he was sound asleep, and she called the police. They got there just as he was waking up and — Jim! I've been had, haven't I?'

'Just one question,' Jim said. 'Did the watch commander talk to you about the report?'

'Yes.'

'Has he ever talked to you about a case before?'

'No.'

'Yeah. I'd say you've been had.'

Jennifer turned it into points with her boss though, and she even turned the joke around on the men who started it. She wrote the story as if it were fact, until she got to the bottom line where she quoted herself, 'And any reporter who'd buy this has to also believe in the Easter Bunny.'

Leo got a good laugh out of it and told her he was glad she saw through it. She wanted to tell him that her new friend at the Sixteenth was really responsible for saving her from it. But Leo had warned her enough about not fraternizing that she thought better of it.

Then she got a friend from the composing room to doll the story up in type as it might appear in the paper, had it laminated, and presented it to the desk officer. It quoted both him and his boss, and the look on his face when he thought it would be in the next day's paper was worth the embarrassment she had suffered in believing it in the first place.

When Jim Purcell was reassigned, after just a couple of months, to the role of Officer Friendly, it might have meant the end of their contact had it not been for Jennifer's independence. She remembered being disappointed the night he told her that he would no longer be on the desk after the end of the month, but still she felt no stirrings. He was just a nice guy, a rare Christian among a rough bunch of men. They knew little about each other, and neither was really supposed to fraternize with the other — though this was only traditional on both sides, not written policy.

Then the night she had car trouble right in front of the station house, she was tempted to run back in and ask for his help.

But that would have been unprofessional. It might have even looked forward.

But she didn't have time to wait for a tow truck, and who knew what garage would send one this time of night anyway? Should she call Bobby and have him come and get her? Who needed the heat that would bring from Leo? Leo didn't care if you were a man or a woman, he always said, 'You've got your job to do and your deadlines to meet and you do it, that's all.'

So she had called a cab, but she didn't use the pay phone in the precinct. She used a phone down the block where she waited for the cab until just after 11:00 p.m. But the car that finally pulled to the curb was not a cab. A man, alone, wound down the passenger side window. She started back toward the station.

'Hey! It's me, Jim! You need a ride?'

She felt foolish. 'No, thanks, Jim. I've got a cab coming. I just called for one.'

'You *called* a cab? You can hail one faster. The called ones never come. C'mon, where you going? I can run you over to the paper.'

She hesitated, then got in.

'What's wrong with your car?'

'I wish I knew. Won't turn over.'

'I'll drop you at the paper, from a block away if you're worried someone will see.' She smiled, 'And then I'll come back here and take a look. Can't be anything serious. Has it been playing up?'

'Not at all.'

'Probably nothing big then.'

'Oh, Jim, no. I can't let you do that. I'll get a garage to look at it tomorrow. If you can just run me to my office, someone can take me home, and I'll work it out, no problem.'

'Forget it. By the time you're off work, I'll be back to pick you up and take you to your car. Fair enough?'

'I really can't let you do that. It's sweet of you, but no.'

'C'mon! My one chance to be a white knight? Don't ruin it for me. Don't forget, I'm gonna be Officer Friendly.'

She laughed and removed her car keys from her key ring for him. He chided her. 'That's right. Hang onto those apartment keys, just like Officer Friendly would advise. Too easy to copy.'

When she got off work that night, she hoped Bobby — a sweet kid, but a climber and sometimes a big mouth — didn't notice that Jim was waiting out in front. Jim took her back to her car and explained the minor problem that had interrupted the ignition. She thanked him profusely. He asked if he could see her again since he wouldn't be seeing her on business much any more.

'I shouldn't,' she said.

'If I was still going to see you every night on duty, I might not have asked you this soon.'

'I'd better not.'

'You'd better.'

'I don't know.'

'I won't beg.'

'I wouldn't want you to.'

'Please, oh please!'

And they both laughed. 'You can call me,' she said finally. 'But no promises.'

'Ah, so it depends on where I'm going to take you. How do you feel about professional wrestling?'

'Are you kidding?'

'Of course.'

'Whew!'

'I was thinking more in terms of a concert at Ravinia.'

'Now that I'd love,' she said.

'Saturday?'

'Saturday.'

There had been many Saturdays since then. And Sundays at his church. And hers. And Friday nights. And last night, He was perfect for what ailed her. He wasn't pushy. He wasn't demanding. He let her talk about Scott. He let her cry.

It almost embarrassed him that he grew to love his Officer Friendly role. 'It's not something I want to do the rest of my life,' he said, 'because I'd still like to land in Homicide eventually, but I *do* like working with kids.'

'I wouldn't think investigating homicides

would be something you'd want to do the rest of your life either,' she said.

'It wouldn't always be pleasant. But it would always be a challenge, and a worthy one. If we believe God is the author of life, we should want to oppose those who take lives.' But she wondered what it would be like to be married to a man who dealt with bodies and blood and murderers all day.

Then she scolded herself for even thinking that way. What Jim Purcell did with his life was his business, and besides, they weren't past the hand-holding stage. No commitments had been made, no love expressed.

Did she love him? She could. She was capable. She might some day. But now? Did she? She wasn't sure. She decided she'd know when she did. She knew one thing: she loved to watch him with kids. With his Sunday school kids, his friends from church. Even with her nieces and nephews.

And though people in both churches and both families had started making assumptions, she and Jim had not even said they wouldn't see other people yet. No one from their respective places of work knew anything about their relationship. They liked each other. A lot. And she thought he probably loved her. He had expressed it in many ways. She missed him when she didn't see him. She was happier when she was with him.

Sounds like love, she thought. *Feels like love.* But she had been through it before. And the loss, even the potential of the loss of one she could hold so dear, scared her, slowed her, made her careful.

Now, as she entered the Sixteenth Precinct on what she sensed was as important a day in police news since she'd been on the beat, she was thinking of Jim and the quiet dinner they had enjoyed. Simultaneously, she reached into her bag for her note pad.

'Good evening, Herb,' she said to Flannigan. 'What've you got? Who can I see?'

'Nothin' and nobody. How's that?'

She started to smile, but he wasn't kidding. 'What's the matter, Herb? Is everything under wraps? You must know by now who was hit. Anybody I know?'

'I can't tell you anything. It's a guy from IAD, and he's brass. He's at Henrotin, and if you tell anybody I tol' you, it's the last thing you'll ever get from me.'

'I appreciate it, Herb. You know I do. Now what was the bust?'

'I'm afraid it was right here in the Sixteenth,' he said. 'And I'm serious, I can't say a word. I wouldn't tell you who if you paid me.'

'Campbell in?'

'He's in, but the official answer is no, if you know what I mean.'

'No way he'll see me?'

'No way.'

Jennifer pursed her lips and headed for the pay phone near the stairs. 'Hi, it's Grey,' she said. 'Let me talk to Leo.'

While she waited for Leo, she was tempted to try Jim at home again and, short of that, asking Flannigan if Jim had been called in for emergency duty.

'Yeah, Jenn!'

'Leo, I'm at the Sixteenth and getting nothing. I'm going over to Henrotin where they've got this Chief of Internal Affairs.'

'Lucas?'

'Is that his name?'

''Course that's his name. You don't have your department directory with you?'

'No.'

'John Lucas. Very big name. Very impressive. Big news if he's been hit. You know this for sure? I'll start a bio.'

'I can't be sure yet if it's Lucas, but it sounds like he's in pretty bad shape, whoever he is. You think I'll get anybody in Public Information this time of night?'

'I doubt it, but it's worth a try. I can only hold page one until three a.m., and I mean three. You call me at quarter to with whatever you've got, and I gotta tell ya, it better be more than you've got now. You know how many were busted?'

'No.'

'Better get to Henrotin. We'll get the arrested officers from the TV or the wires.

Concentrate on the shot cop, and Bobby'll track down the rest.'

I'll bet he will, Jennifer thought, feeling as if she had failed already. She didn't want help. She didn't want to be reminded what she'd forgotten. She didn't want to have to concentrate on just one aspect of the story, regardless of the time pressure. She was angry.

Pushing open the glass door to the lobby she called to Flannigan. 'Give me the number for Public Information, fast!'

He didn't have time to think about it. He peeled open the dog-eared department directory and yelled out the number. When the switchboard downtown answered, Jennifer identified herself and asked for the Public Information Director. 'No, it's not an emergency,' she said with more sarcasm than she should have.

She was told he was unavailable. 'Are you telling me he's not in the office? Because I don't think his wife will be too thrilled to take a call right now, especially if he isn't home.'

'He's here, but unavailable.'

'Tell him it's the *Chicago Day,* and don't tell me he isn't out talking to the broadcast people right now. Tell him I just need him for a second.'

Jennifer looked at her watch and panicked. If she was just getting information that Bobby could get elsewhere and she missed the one part of the story Leo told her to stay on, she'd be in big trouble. She tapped her foot impatiently and began preparing herself to run to her car as soon as she talked to the Public Information Director.

'This is Nelson, sir. What is it?'

'First of all, I'm not a sir, but don't apologize. I'm Jennifer Grey with the *Day* and —'

'Yes, I've seen your stuff —'

'Good, I need to know what Sixteenth Precinct officers were arrested this morning.'

'I'm sorry, Grey, but those announcements don't come from this office. They are always handled by Internal Affairs, and I'm afraid they're incapacitated at this moment.'

'Because John Lucas is in intensive care at Henrotin?'

'Who told you that?'

'You did. I was just guessing. Thanks, Nelson.'

'You're welcome.'

'Just one more thing. Where are the arrested officers being booked?'

'Down here.'

'Can I come?'

'Suit yourself. But we won't even be giving out the names.'

You might not be, Jennifer thought, *but somebody down there is always eager to tell what they know.*

4 Jennifer sped to Henrotin Hospital on the Near North Side and debated parking in the emergency lane. Instead, she parked as close as she could to the door and popped her press card on the dashboard. *That's one way to beg for a ticket,* she thought.

She was among the press latecomers in the casualty department, asking all the questions everyone else had already tried. And getting the same answer. No comment. She walked the corridors and asked doctors, nurses, assistants, and cleaners if they knew anything at all about the condition of the man in intensive care.

They had been briefed well. That or they'd been through this before, Henrotin being a popular site for the most common emergencies in the world of crime that surrounded it. Jennifer spotted a pay phone and dialled casualty. She could hear the nurse on duty live in one ear and by phone in the other. She turned toward the wall so the effect wouldn't be reversed.

'This is Jennifer Grey calling from the Near North Side,' she said. 'I must know immediately if you called the morgue and whether you will be transferring Mr. Lucas's body there?'

'I didn't call the morgue,' she said. 'I don't believe Mr. Lucas has expired, ma'am.'

'Is that correct? I understood that he may have already died.'

'One moment please.'

A male voice came on. 'This is Dr. Burris. May I help you?'

'I need to know the condition of Mr. Lucas as soon as you can put me in touch with someone in authority.'

'Well, we'll be releasing this to the press at about three-thirty a.m. anyway if there has been no change: His condition is grave. He is suffering from wounds to the abdomen and the cardiovascular system. He has not been conscious since the time of the shooting. We have been able to remove only one bullet at this time, and further surgery must be postponed until his condition stabilizes, probably not for several hours. All vital signs are weak.'

'What kind of chance would you give him, Doctor?'

'One in ten.'

'Thank you.'

Jennifer phoned the news in to Leo and headed downtown. There'd be no one falling for an innocent phone call down at headquarters, however straightforward. She had never been able to justify lying, which Leo felt was fair. She always told the party her name and what she wanted to know, emphasizing the urgency of it and appealing to their rank. If they asked her more specifically why she wanted to know, she told them, but they seldom asked.

Jennifer arrived at 2:30 a.m. Again she was a latecomer. Her colleagues pressed around Public Information Director Nelson, who was asking how many were on a hot deadline. 'I am,' Jennifer called, remembering the days when it was all she could do to muster the courage to ask a simple question at a press conference.

'I oughta head for the phone right now,' one of her competitors quipped. 'The *Day* stayin' open after sundown is front page stuff!'

Everyone guffawed, but Jennifer ignored them and talked directly to Nelson again. 'I'm looking at fifteen minutes,' she said. 'I'll take whatever you've got.'

'All I have is four names.'

'We've all got the names,' she said, taking

a chance, assuming Leo and Bobby had been able to get that much. She lost the gamble. Everyone turned and stared, then shouted at Nelson, demanding to know why she had information that they didn't.

He held up both hands. 'She's bluffing,' he said. 'No one has the names because I just got them myself. Now, Grey, the names are all I have except a few details. If you've already got what I'm about to give, you might as well head back to the *Day*.' She stared him down.

'Now, then, ladies and gentlemen, a few ground rules. I have very brief, very sketchy reports for you. I will read them verbatim the way I have been instructed. I will not be able to comment further on them. I have nothing more on the arrests themselves, and I cannot release the names of the arresting officers.

'I can tell you that at around midnight, the Internal Affairs Division of the Chicago Police Department made four arrests of police personnel, charging them with trafficking in controlled substances. These four arrested officers are being held without bail in this building. The police commissioner is releasing the following statement: "These arrests come after lengthy preparation by the Internal Affairs Division. However, we will consider the arrested officers innocent until proven guilty. Any so found will not only be dismissed from the police force but will be prosecuted to the full extent of the law.''

'That statement was prepared in advance. With the wounding of IAD Chief John Lucas, the commissioner has added this: ''Our prayers are with the wounded officer and his family.''

'Lucas's is the only name I can give you from the list of arresting officers. He was critically wounded during the arrest of Lieutenant Frank Akeley of the Sixteenth Precinct. The arrest was made in the car-park of The Illusion bar on Wells Street. I know none of the details except that Chief Lucas was hit three times by small calibre ammunition and is in intensive care at Henrotin Hospital at this time. No one else was injured.'

'Did this Akeley shoot him?'

'I am not at liberty to comment on that.'

'How many officers were at the scene?'

'I do not know.'

'Is he expected to live?'

'I'm sorry, gentlemen — and ladies. As I told you, this is all I have. Now there is more on the other arrests, if you'd care to hear it.'

'Yeah, but you got stats on Akeley?'

'Yes. White, male, age fifty-nine, five feet eleven inches, thirteen stone, three pounds. The highest ranking officer arrested this evening. An employee of the City of Chicago for thirty-two years.'

'Family?'

'That's all I have.'

'Stats on Lucas?'

'Yes. White, male, age fifty-six, six feet two inches, thirteen stone, eight pounds. Thirty-year employee.'

'Family?'

'Wife, four grown-up daughters.'

'The other arrested officers included Sergeant William Much, also Sixteenth Precinct. Arrested at his home on the West Side. He's married, two teenage sons and a younger daughter. White, male, age forty-three, six feet four inches, eighteen stone, thirteen pounds. Employed by Chicago PD for nineteen years.'

'Who arrested him?' Laughter.

'I don't have that information.'

'Is the arresting officer still alive?' More laughter. Nelson ignored it.

'That name sounds familiar. Has he ever been up on charges before?'

'No, but we've released stories about him from our office twice in the last year. One — which none of you used — was a feature on the fact that he's our singing policeman. The other — which you all used — was that he was our biggest policeman and that he had been ordered to lose weight before the end of this year.'

'How's he doing? He gonna make it?'

Nelson was not amused. He looked as if he wanted to say he didn't have that information, but of course he had the file on the old feature story. He ignored the question anyway.

'Arrested on duty, and again, I am not at liberty to give you the name of the arresting officer, was Patrol Officer Trudy Janus, white, female, age twenty-seven, five feet five inches, ten stone. Single. Employed here three years.'

'First female in that precinct?'

'Yes.'

'First female officer ever arrested?'

'I believe so. Better not quote me on that.'

'Any of these resist arrest?'

'No comment.'

'Did more than one resist arrest?'

'No.'

'There's one more?'

'James Purcell, a specially assigned Patrol Officer, white, male, age twenty-nine, six feet one inch, twelve stone, two pounds, six-year employee. Arrested at his Near North Side apartment.'

Jennifer squinted and stared unblinking at Nelson. Her throat had tightened at the first mention of Jim's name, and her desperate hope that it was another James Purcell was dashed immediately with the cold recitation of his statistics. The numbness that had plagued her after the death of her husband swept over her once more.

There has to be a mistake, she thought as she stiffly backed away from the scene. She was terrified for Jim and what he must be going through. She didn't want to face the news. It was too stark, too impersonal, too awful. It took her back three years to the phone call that asked her if she were Mrs. Scott Alan Grey. She knew by the way she had been asked that something terrible had happened.

The caller had identified himself as a state trooper and asked cordially if she would be home for the next half hour or so and could he please call in for a moment. She had known so certainly then that she called her father and told him to come to Arlington Heights, that Scott had been killed, and that she needed her parents.

She never once doubted the truth of her conviction, and, of course, she was right. She made it easy for the young trooper. 'How did it happen?' she asked, refusing his suggestion that she sit down.

'Multiple car accident, icy roads. No one's fault.'

'Anyone else hurt?'

'Yes, ma'am. No other fatalities, however.'

'Could you stay with me for a half hour or so until my parents arrive?'

'Of course. Would you like me to call them for you? It wouldn't be any trouble.'

'They're on their way.'

Jennifer's first thought as she backed through the door now was to stop at the pay phone and call her father. But she couldn't. There were too many reasons she couldn't. She wanted to shut this out, to wake up from it, to be done with it.

Her deadline was closing in, and she was a newspaper woman. She was not a woman in love. She was not a person with a second chance at life. She was Leo Stanton's ace police reporter. Maybe she had wobbly legs, and maybe she was on the verge of hysterics. But a grown woman doesn't wake up her father in the middle of the night when she has a job to do.

So she phoned Leo. While the rest of the pack were running for other phones and howling about Officer Friendly being a drug dealer and 'Wasn't this the guy who wanted to get out of vice control because he wasn't old enough? No, he found out there wasn't as much money in it!' Jennifer told Leo that he'd better get another hour from the pressmen.

'I told you, Jenn, three means three. We go to press in a few minutes. What's the matter with you anyway? You sound strange.'

'I'm sitting on the biggest story of my career, Leo. Trust me. I'll come straight in and give you a lead story for page one in the first draft. If you don't hold the press for this piece, we'll be blown out by all the other news media.'

'You know what you're asking, Jennifer?'

'Leo, I asked myself what you would do in this situation, and that's what I'm doing.'

Stanton laughed a rueful laugh. 'I can't argue with that. I'll get you a four o'clock pressrun; you get in here and give me the story.'

Jennifer knew she couldn't drive, so she grabbed a cab and paid him in advance so she could jump out when he slid up to the night entrance at the *Day*. She hid her face in her hands and tried to control her sobs, but she couldn't.

The public has a right to hear this story whether these people are guilty or innocent, she told herself over and over. *He just has to be innocent! He couldn't! He wouldn't! I know him too well! Who am I kidding? I don't know him at all. I've been taken in. He used me. But the story can't be vindictive. It has to be straight. It has to be the piece I would write if I'd never heard of the man. God, don't let this be true! Please make it all be a mistake!*

She hurried into the city room, shedding her coat and her bag and reading her notes as she walked. Bobby approached and handed her a story. 'Leo let me take a shot at the Lucas piece. What do you think?'

She sensed Bobby's gloating and tried to scan the piece through her tears.

John Lucas, 56, is fighting for his life
at Henrotin Hospital this morning

after suffering multiple gunshot
wounds during a midnight arrest on
the Near North Side.

The long-time veteran with a
reputation for incorruptibility was
personally handling the arrest of
Chicago Police Lieutenant Frank
Akeley, 59, who allegedly opened fire
in the car-park of....

'Yeah, yeah, I think that'll be OK,'
Jennifer managed, wondering which story
Leo would lead with. Not that she cared. In
a selfish, protective way, she could wish
that he would bury her story. She would beg
him to leave her name off it, maybe even
threaten to leave if he didn't comply.

Leo gave her a puzzled look, and she
slowed as she passed his desk, wondering if
she didn't owe him some sort of an explanation. He started to pull his cigar from his
lips, then remembered the time and just left
it. He clicked his fingers and pointed to her
video display terminal, and she kept walking.

It was warm in the city room, or was it
just Jennifer? She pulled her sweater over
her head and sat, still steaming, in her
blouse. She set up her note pad next to the
machine while trying to remove her boots
with her free hand. No luck.

She bent down and put her head under
the desk to get a better vantage point from

which to attack the zippers. While in that ridiculous position, it hit her what she was about to do.

She was going to write a story for the fastest growing newspaper in Chicago that would end a man's career for ever, guilty or innocent. *But the story won't, can't, say he's guilty,* she reasoned.

And the facts will be broadcast on radio and television and printed in all the other papers anyway. There's no way I can protect him. And why should I? Because I know he can't be guilty, that's why. Don't I? And either way, it's a story. A valid story. Either way, it's news that he was arrested. And there's irony in his present assignment.

She had to do it. Leo stared at her taking so long to take off her boots. She'd been running since Bobby had called her just before 1:00 a.m. She needed a shower. She needed a shampoo. She needed a change of clothes. She needed a bed.

What she wanted was her parents. *Why do I have to be such a baby?* Her dad had told her that it took more of a woman to admit she needed someone than to need someone and pretend she didn't.

That was sage advice, as usual, from Dad. But this time it didn't fit. Because this time what she wanted and what she needed were two different things. She would have said to herself, and did, that she wanted her parents. She wanted to go home to Rockford, home to her old bedroom, home to long days of sleeping her cares away.

But what she needed? What she really needed? If she'd had her choice of all the options in the world, would she really go home? No. She would go to Jim. She would tell him she believed him, whatever his story was.

And she knew when she even let that thought enter her head that it was ludicrous. It was the thought of a crazy woman. It was the kind of thing a woman in love would say. *I love him,* she told herself. *I finally know that I love him, and I have every reason to believe he's a criminal.*

Surer of her love than of his innocence, she straightened up, gave one hard glance back at Leo — who had been about to tell her to make good on her page one story or look for a new job — and turned to her machine.

Her tears began afresh, and as they rolled down her face, she punched in the toughest story she would ever write. Knowing it would go out over the *Day* syndicate as well, she datelined it Chicago and began:

James Purcell, 29, the Sunday school teaching Chicago policeman who begged a transfer from his unsavoury assignment to the Vice Control Division early this year and has been serving as Officer Friendly in the area's schools, was one of four 16th Precinct police officers arrested early this morning and charged with buying and selling illegal drugs.

In the quadruple arrests that took place at four separate locations simultaneously, Internal Affairs Division Chief John Lucas was critically wounded. (See separate story.) The other three arrests, including Purcell, veteran Sergeant William Much, 43, and Patrol Officer Trudy Janus, 27, were without incident....

5 It was all Jennifer could do to finish the article, she wanted so badly to see Jim.

But at police headquarters she was faced with a brick wall. 'No, Jennifer, absolutely not, no way. Sorry.'

'What're you talking about, Bradley?' she pleaded with the lanky, dark deskman. 'You've taken me in to see your *own* prisoners before!'

'Maybe that's why I got stuck on desk duty, Jenn. I've got orders. Nobody sees these four except their lawyers. That's it, so don't beg.'

'Can you give him a message for me?'

Bradley appeared to consider it. 'Not without clearance from my boss, Jennifer.'

'How long would that take?'

'I dunno. He works the day shift, and I ain't gonna call him at home. I could leave it for him.'

'Forget it,' she said, trying to keep from screaming. 'Is there really no way I can get in there for a few minutes, if I promise to keep your name out of it?'

'C'mon, Jennifer, I told you not to beg. I'm in charge of the keys until tomorrow, so there's no way anyone can keep my name out of anything if you get in there. I'm sorry, OK?'

Jennifer couldn't speak, not even to thank him for listening to her. She trudged to her car, fighting tears and suddenly feeling the fatigue that the last few hectic hours had made her ignore. She banged both hands against the steering wheel, fighting the sobs that were just beneath the surface.

She made a conscious decision not to cry. She wanted to be with Jim, but she couldn't be, and that was that. Sleep was what she needed.

The morning papers and the radio news programmes made the most of the arrests, speculating on how many police officers would wind up indicted when all the results were in.

They had great fun, of course, with the singing policeman — the biggest man on the force — being brought down by the scandal. But their ire was reserved for Jim Purcell, the one they said had played the 'Officer Friendly' image to the hilt.

While hearts bled for John Lucas, and hourly hospital reports sounded worse and worse, Jennifer sat in her apartment unable to turn away from the radio call-in programmes. People who knew nothing except what they're read in the paper, and — she knew many of them had read only her article — ranted and raved about the fact that 'this man, or at least this person who calls himself a man, spends his days telling kids that the police department is on their side and spends his nights selling heroin to the same children!'

Leo had reluctantly complied with her ultimatum, and she wondered if she would have had the fortitude to follow through with her threat to resign if he had crossed her. After hearing the diatribes all morning, she knew she would have. Still, even without the byline, Jim Purcell would know who wrote those stories.

And why was she still worried about that? If it had all been a mistake and he was cleared, he'd have to understand, wouldn't he? Wouldn't any sane adult know that the story was news? That it would have appeared everywhere else anyway? And that she and the *Day* would have looked suspicious for not covering it?

But the more she thought about it, the more she knew that it was something else that was bothering her. It was the possibility that it was all true. That she had been duped by a con man second to none. If she was wrong about Jim, she could never trust another human being as long as she lived.

The man was special. He reminded her of her own father. The kindness, the under-standing, the gentleness, the insight. Could a person be that confused, that deceived, that totally swept away by someone?

It was inconceivable! She wracked her brain for clues to a side of him she never knew. He was idealistic. He was sometimes unrealistic. Yet he was responsible. He was one of those who volunteered for unpopular duty, working weekends and holidays when the family men wanted to arrange days off.

Were there times when he was unavail-able, and she didn't know why or he didn't explain? She could think of none. There seemed to be a lot of meetings, staff meet-ings. And not always at the precinct house. Could that have been when he was doing his dirty work? She had no reason to believe that.

No reason except for the sketchy reports coming out of Internal Affairs that this sur-veillance had been under way for longer than Jim had been in the precinct. She decided she could live with the bad news more easily than with no news. If she could find out for sure that he was the scoundrel the stories implied, she would deal with the pain, the remorse, the grief of it, the same way she had dealt with the loss of Scott.

There were similarities; of course there were. Especially after the realization at her keyboard in the wee hours that she was indeed in love with Jim. Memories of their praying together stabbed through her. *Could he be a phony? Is it possible? Could a man drag God into a sham? I suppose a real pro could.*

But Jim was sincere in his distaste for the work he'd been assigned in the Vice Control Division. Having to play up to prostitutes and pay off informants. Deciding which crime was more important and letting the small-time criminal go, and maybe even helping him or her out, in exchange for the bigger prey.

He said he'd been raised straight and had never really been in serious trouble, certainly not involving the seamier side of life. He was not only repulsed by the after-dark world of Chicago, but he also found himself fascinated and even tempted by parts of it. He found himself thinking thoughts he'd never entertained before, seeing pictures in his mind he wondered if he could ever erase.

He wasn't a prude, he'd said. It wasn't that he didn't know what went on behind closed doors. But he'd always appreciated the counsel of an older Christian policeman who had said that a Christian officer 'must be fully acquainted with sin but not partake of it'.

This vice control business was for someone else, according to Jim. And when Jennifer heard his view of it, she had to agree. There were bad, horrible, awful sides to other parts of police work too — like trying to solve grisly murders. But while they, too, left memory pictures that needed cleansing, they didn't begin to work on a young man's imagination or make him remember the alluring sights of the underworld. And only a blind man could deny that they were there.

No man would admit to his family that he wanted all that went with the action in the sleazy strip clubs and hangouts. There was filth and disease and burned-out men and women. But could the same man say that there weren't sights that appealed to his lower nature, possibilities that excited his fantasies?

Jim, Jennifer felt, had decided he didn't need that kind of input. He was admitting to the world that it took either a stronger man for the work or one who didn't care about the purity of his thought life.

Jim had told Jennifer more than he had told any other reporter — because he was telling her off-the-record as a friend, even though he never stipulated such. He had told her that his reason was his faith in

Christ, his eagerness to do and to be and to become all that God wanted him to.

Somehow she couldn't make those lofty ideals fit the worst con man in the business. But maybe they were what made him the best.

She rose from the couch, where fits of exhausted sleep left her more tired than refreshed, and shuffled to the phone. She called Leo at home. 'Well, I guess we've got another paper to put out for tomorrow morning,' she said.

'Yeah, I suppose we do, Jenn. You all right?'

'I think so.'

'We're going to have to talk about it, you know that, don't you?'

'Talk about what?'

'C'mon, Jenn. You're talking to Leo. And Leo knows. You ought to know that by now. But better than that, just like your mum, Leo cares. Thing is, you can fool Mum. You can't fool Leo.'

'I know. I'm sorry.'

'Don't be sorry. Just talk to me. What's happening with you, Jennifer? Why are you taking this story so hard? You get too close to these people or something? Know them too well? I warned you about taking sides, about seeing yourself as one of the cops instead of a reporter, standing between them and the readers.'

'Yeah, well, maybe that was it, Leo. It does hurt to see people hurt.'

'But *they* hurt people, Jennifer. It was *their* fault. You've got to see that, to separate yourself from them, to see the public's side. If you're going to be a bleeding-heart cheerleader for the cops, you're no good to us in your job.'

'Maybe you're right. Maybe I'm no good in the job.'

'We both know that's nonsense. You called me. You said we've got another paper to put out. That tells me you're ready for an assignment today. I was going to give you a day off, but if you're ready —'

'You were? You were going to give me a break? I don't know what to think about that, Leo. What am I supposed to think about that?'

'Since when are you asking me what you're supposed to think? That'll be the day.'

'No, I just mean, are you feeling sorry for me? Wondering if I can handle the job? What?'

'You worked hard last night, and it was getting to you. It showed. You can't deny that.'

'It showed in my piece?'

'No, your story was as nice as you've done since you've been with me. But you do a great job, you cry at your desk, you don't

want your name on the story. I'm no psychi-
atrist, Jenn, but I've got to think my star
reporter needs a day to herself.'

'That's thoughtful, Leo. But no, I think I'll
do better working than sitting around here
all day thinking.'

'You're sure?'

'Yeah.'

'You want an assignment?'

'Sure.'

'You know it's going to be right in the
middle of this Internal Affairs bust.'

'Sure.'

'Well, there *have* been a few develop-
ments I'd like you to check out. First, the
names of the arresting officers have leaked
out. Bobby's got 'em at the office. You can
try to contact them. Second, Lucas has
taken a turn for the worse. The doctors are
saying it's only a matter of time. Third, no
one but their lawyers is allowed in to see
the four busted cops, but get this: only three
of them even have lawyers. Akeley, who's
been formally charged now with resisting
arrest, assault with a deadly weapon, and
attempted murder, has procured this
Williams, you remember the guy?'

'The Williams who represented the City
of Chicago in federal court? Big stuff.'

'Yeah, that's the guy. But I have a feeling
that with the testimony of two of his own
precinct cops against him, Akeley's going to

need more than Williams. Anyway, it appears this Bill Much, the —'

'Sergeant.'

'Yeah, Much is broke and is using a public defender. That's worth a few laughs when you think about it. A defender of the public violates the public trust, then hires a public defender to defend himself against the public. It's too good. But not funny. I'm sorry. I forgot how you're reacting to this.'

'It's all right.'

'OK, Janus has a guess-what lawyer?'

'A woman.'

'You got it.'

'A known feminist defender.'

'Right again.'

'You're telling me the fourth defendant doesn't have counsel yet?'

'That's the story, Jenn. He isn't going to have counsel. What's his name?'

'Purcell.'

'Right. This James Purcell, the Holy Joe, has waived his right to a lawyer.'

'Temporarily, surely.'

'Maybe. But what's his game? That's what I want you to find out. What would you think of visiting his church? Talking to his pastor, some of his friends? They'll say they're shocked and all that, never would have thought it. Maybe they'll stick up for him. But go deeper. Find out what the parents of the kids he teaches in Sunday school think about letting their kids stay in his class if he gets out on bail. Or if the church will let him keep his class. What do the people think? I don't suppose you could get to one of the kids, but that would be interesting too. My guess is the kids will not believe it yet.'

'Do you believe it, Leo?'

'I missed that.'

'Do you believe Purcell is guilty?'

Leo swore. 'They're all guilty, Jenn. Once in a great while there'll be smoke with no fire. But when you're talking official corruption, your cops and your politicians and your government employees, uh-uh. In the *Day*, just like in every other rag that wants to be fair and ethical, our pieces will be full of alleged this and allegedly that and all the rest. But let me tell you something: the alleged Akeley who allegedly shot the alleged chief of the alleged IAD is going to be in a heap of alleged trouble if his victim allegedly dies. Yeah, Jenn, they're all as guilty as sin, and when you've been on this beat long — in fact, probably after this coverage right here — you'll never doubt it again.'

Jennifer was silent, trying to keep from crying.

'C'mon, Jennifer. Be realistic. I don't want to be such a cynic any more than anyone else, but you've got to snap out of this Pollyanna business. I like a reporter who can be optimistic and look on the bright side of things. But there is no bright side to a cop scandal. Talking to a guy's Sunday school class might seem a little crass. But did you ever see a story of a mass murderer that doesn't carry quotes from the people he grew up with, people who taught him?'

'I guess not.'

'Of course you didn't. Now what do you want to take today? You get first choice of course. Bobby and I'll take the rest, along with a couple of stringers we're borrowing from the newsroom.'

'I'll tell you what I want to do, if you don't mind, Leo. I'd like to take you up on your offer of a day off. I could really use the time.'

This time Leo was silent.

'Is that OK?'

'Sure, Jenn. How much time you need?'

'Just a day. I'll see you tomorrow afternoon.'

'You going to get some rest, kid?'

'I don't know. I might go and see my parents in Rockford.'

'I'll be thinking about you. Give me a call if you need me, huh?'

'Thanks, Leo. Thanks a lot.'

6 Though she was hounded by it all the drive, Jennifer couldn't decide what significance there was to Jim's decision not to procure a lawyer. Was it lack of money? Could she help? Should she? Would she have to leave her job first? What if she was wrong about him and left her job to help him, all in vain? They'd both be ruined.

She wouldn't have thought twice about sacrificing her career for him if he was innocent. But how could she be sure? What was she saying? That she loved him enough to sacrifice for him, yet she didn't know if he was innocent?

She saw the familiar mailbox with her parents' names — George and Lillian Knight — and pulled into the drive, realizing immediately that she had made a mistake. She had forgotten that her mother had invited her older brother, Drew, his nagging wife, Francene, and their three toddlers for a week.

Drew she loved. Francene she tolerated, trying to forgive her nasal twang (a gift from birth) and her constant badgering of her husband and the kids by blaming it on the burden of trying to manage such a household.

Tolerating Francene was a full-time job even without the kids crying, wetting, fighting, and running through every conversation in the house. When Jennifer's mother and dad saw her in the driveway, they ran out.

Her mother had that look of joy that accompanies the thought of having most of her family together. 'Hi, Darling,' she called, embracing Jennifer. 'Now if only Tracy could be here!'

George Knight, however, had the concerned look that went with having read the *Morning Star* and knowing something about his daughter that he had not yet told his wife. And Jennifer could tell.

'How are you, Jenny?' he asked, taking her hands in his and looking deep into her eyes. He was the only person who called her Jenny any more, and it always transported her back to treehouses and sandboxes and long walks in the woods. He called her

Jenny right through high school when they had their one-to-one talks that would go on till after midnight.

He'd never said she was his favourite, but she knew. And he loved her, he always said, even when she was being difficult. That always got to her. She'd be moody or terrorize her mother with that temper of hers, and he would sit her down and give her the Dutch-uncle routine. She'd sulk and pout and refuse to admit she'd been wrong. She'd try the silent treatment, defying him with her eyes, and he'd say in a way that endeared him to her for ever: 'You can't make me not like you, Jenny Knight. And you can't stay angry with your old dad because I love you even when you're difficult.'

And if she'd been so moody that she couldn't force a smile, she'd break down and cry, and he'd hold her. He never forced an apology out of her. But after she had seen herself in contrast to this sensitive, gentle man, she wanted more than anything to be like him, to get things right again, to forgive and forget and be forgiven.

Now he was staring into her eyes and asking her how she was, and she knew he knew what was going on. Somehow she sensed that he had not told the others. Mum wasn't a newspaper reader, unless Jennifer had written the story. Drew was way above front-page news, always with his nose in some science magazine. And Francene hadn't sat still long enough to read a paragraph since her firstborn, her four-year-old wonder, had come along.

'Oh, Drew!' came the dreaded whine. 'Look who's here! Hi, Jennifer. How are you?'

Jennifer saw her father's face soften into an understanding smile. She rolled her eyes. 'Hi, Fran! Good to see you.'

'How long can you stay?' Mrs. Knight wanted to know.

'Not long,' Jennifer said, having wished she could stay overnight, but realizing now that it would do her psyche and her problem no good to try to survive a household of relatives.

'Well, come in and sit down,' her mother said. 'Have a bite.'

Drew pecked her on the cheek as she came through the door, and he rounded up all the kids to say hi to Aunt Jennifer. They came, kicking and screaming, performing their duties and heading off to see what more havoc could be wreaked.

When her mother was at the stove, Jennifer's father leaned close. 'Where's your head?' he whispered.

'Right here,' she said, pointing to her heart. He nodded with an I-thought-so-look. 'I forgot they were going to be here,' she said, and he nodded again. 'What I really need, Dad, is a long talk with you.'

'I think we can work that out,' he said. 'What do you think, Mum?'

'What's that, Dear?'

'You think Jenny and I could sneak away for an hour or so before dinner?'

'Sure. Be back by five-thirty though.'

The frozen path that led to the woods behind the house seemed so much smaller than it had the last time they had walked there. Fatigue had set in, and Jennifer needed to rest. They sat on dry stumps in the middle of a tiny alcove, and she wondered aloud what her mother would think when she read about Jim.

'Let me worry about that,' her father said. 'I'm more concerned with what *you're* thinking right now.'

So she told him. The whole story. How she heard. What she felt. What she did. What she said to Leo. That she knew she loved Jim, and mostly, that she was surer of her love than of his innocence.

She had finished, and, as was her father's custom, he didn't respond immediately. He just sat. Thinking. Waiting. Giving her a chance to restate anything she had not said the way she wanted to. Letting her own words echo in her ears to see how they sounded out in the open rather than in the echoing valleys of her mind.

She wasn't tempted to ask him what he thought. She knew he'd tell her. When he had sifted it through, he would ask her a few questions she hadn't thought to ask herself. He would give her insight she could have had on her own. He would lead her to her own decisions, never trying to force one on her.

It hadn't always been that way. He wasn't perfect. He had tried so hard to hold onto her when she was an adolescent that he had, a time or two, tried to push his will onto her. It never worked, and they both learned from it. But he was so eminently forgivable, if for no other reason than that line about loving her even when she was difficult.

'What will it do to your love for him if you find that he's guilty?' he said at last.

Jennifer couldn't answer. As she had silently predicted, it was something she hadn't considered. His guilt she had considered. How would it affect her feelings for him? She had assumed, she thought, that her love for him was dependent upon his character.

'I think I love the man I thought he was,' she said. 'Does that make sense?'

'Do you think it does?'

'I know it sounds conditional, but that was all I knew of him. You can only love what you know, can't you?'

'Can you?'

'I learned things about Scott after we were married, and I loved him in spite of some of those.'

'And vice-versa?'

'Of course. But, Dad, those were little things. Irritations, idiosyncrasies. Not character things. Not dishonest things.'

He looked at her without speaking.

'I'm saying my love is conditional, aren't I?'

He smiled.

'Can't my love be conditional? Is there something wrong with falling out of love if you've been betrayed, if someone is not only not what you thought they were, but the exact opposite?'

'Are you asking me or telling me?'

'I'm asking you, Dad, but I know how you counsel. You'll tell me it's not what *you* think that matters, but what *I* think. But I'm so confused right now that I need some feedback from you. What kind of crazy lady doesn't know she loves someone until he's in trouble? I mean, I know now that I was in love with him before without realizing it. But why does it hit me with such force when it appears he's everything I hate in a person?'

'You're not loving him because he's in jail, Jenny. You're loving him for the same reason you loved him those last few times you brought him up here.'

'You knew?'

'Of course, we could tell. You can't hide something like that. Other people always know before the stricken one knows. But now maybe you know for sure because he needs you. If he was hurt or missing or victimized in some other way, it would have hit you the same way. It's not so paradoxical as it seems.'

'But what will it do to my love for him if I find out he's guilty?'

'That question sounds familiar.'

'He could be, you know, Dad.'

'He could be guilty?'

'Of course. The odds are that he is. They've been watching that precinct for so long. They don't make arrests like that without something solid. Oh, I've been through all this.'

'That's all right. You'll go through it a lot more before you come to any conclusions. You'd better just keep kicking it around in your head until it settles into place.'

'If I had to answer you now —'

'Which you don't.'

'I know, and I appreciate that. But if I had to answer you now, I'd say that finding out he was guilty would spoil my love for him. My love is built on trust and faith. If he had fallen, made a mistake, taken a wrong turn, that would be one thing. I think I could love him through that. But if he's been involved in this since before we met and has been living a lie before me all this time — then, no, that would be the end.'

'You couldn't forgive him?'

'Ah, touché. I don't know.'

Her father fell silent again.

'I know that's what God would do, Dad. But I'm not God.'

'No, none of us are God. But we're supposed to be imitators of Him.'

'You are.'

'I'm not, Jenny. But it *is* my goal.'

'Mine too. But I'm not there. I can't judge Jim. I can't know his heart, his motives, his sincerity. I'm afraid if I knew he was guilty, that he had been thumbing his nose at my pure love — and I don't apologize for calling it that — then I would find it very difficult to accept an apology. Unless it was somehow very convincing.'

'What does that make you think of, Jenny?'

'I know.'

'Do you ever wonder if God believes you're sincere after you've, what did you call it, thumbed your nose at His pure love?'

'Yes. And there were times when I knew I *wasn't* sincere, and I knew He knew it, and it made me feel so guilty that I got sincere fast.'

George Knight smiled broadly and wrapped an arm around his daughter's waist as they walked back. 'You've got a lot of thinking to do, girl.' She nodded. 'I do have one little bit of advice for you, though.'

She stopped, surprised. 'This is a switch.'

'I won't say anything if you don't want me to,' he said, 'but I believe you really are confused and at the end of yourself. I don't mind telling you, I haven't seen you this troubled since —'

'Since Scott.'

'Yes.'

'I want your advice, Dad, Whatever it is, I want it.'

'I can't tell you whether Jim is guilty or innocent. No one can. That will have to be proven. But all I want to tell you — and you can throw it out or take it or whatever you want — is that I think you'll handle this thing better if you give Jim the benefit of the doubt until you know for sure.'

'I might look like a fool in the end.'

'Maybe. But if he's a phony, he's already made a fool of you. And you'll have a lot of company. I like the man. Your mother likes him. The people in his church love him. You love him. If he's betrayed us all, then you can know it and go on from there.

'But what if he hasn't, Jenny? You can only gain by giving him the benefit of the doubt. Believe with all your heart that he's innocent. That there's an explanation. That it'll all work out in the end. If you're wrong, you were just prolonging how wrong you'd been from the start. But if you're right, you'll be glad you stuck by him.'

They walked on in silence for several minutes. 'My boss says the opposite, you know,' she said finally.

'Doesn't surprise me. But he's talking to

you as a newspaper woman. What was his line? Where there's smoke and all that? That's true enough. We both know the odds are against you. You said it yourself. You do your reporting job the best way you know how. But as God's person, as my daughter, as Jim's love, you believe in him until you're proved wrong. It's a much better angle from which to work, don't you think?'

'Don't I think? No, why should I think when I've got a dad like you to do my thinking for me?' And she hugged him.

When they got to the back garden, Lillian Knight was at the door. 'Jenn! Your boss called. Wants you to call him right away. Says he's sorry to bother you, but it's urgent.'

7 In person, Leo Stanton ranted and raved and used his expressions and gestures to make his points. On the phone, when he was really angry, he was terse, cold, impersonal.

'Jennifer,' he said, 'I think you'd better get back here as quickly as possible.'

'What is it, Leo?'

'We can discuss it when you get here. When may I expect you?'

'You want me to leave right now?'

'I think that would be wise.'

'Give me about an hour and a half then.'

'Thank you,' he said, hanging up without another word.

Jennifer tried to treat her fast departure as a minor crisis at the office, but in the car the mystery nearly drove her mad. Who did Leo think he was, demanding that she come back from her parents' without telling her what was going on? Had Lucas died? Did they simply need her at the office? Was that it? Couldn't he have just said that?

Maybe it was more. Maybe Leo had found out about her and Jim. She hoped not. That would ruin the plan that had been taking shape in her mind from the moment — just minutes before — when her father encouraged her to give Jim the benefit of the doubt.

She hadn't had time to sort it all out, but she agreed that taking the positive approach would save her — or at least postpone — a lot of grief. She'd be good for nothing in any effort to help clear Jim if she continually tormented herself with doubt.

She wanted to inform Leo of her chats with Jim — not of their relationship exactly, but of the discussions they'd had about his philosophy of life. She'd write these, she thought, in feature form, just providing curious readers with background on one of the arrested officers.

She didn't know what Leo would think. Worse, she didn't know what Jim would think. He didn't want a lawyer for some reason; maybe he didn't want her defending him either. Of course, he had told her all those things as a friend. But he hadn't ever *said* they were off-the-record, and he knew he was talking to a reporter, didn't he?

She knew she wasn't making sense, but

this was something that could only help Jim. Readers who didn't believe him would have a field day — that's how she would sell it to Leo. A story about a guy who still maintains his innocence in the face of serious charges. Leo should love that.

All the while, of course, she would be hoping and praying that Jim's boyish honesty would come through and that someone would be convinced. Maybe the readers would get behind him again, the way they had when he took his stand against some of the things required of him as a Vice Control Division undercover cop.

But when Jennifer slowed to a stop and wound down her window to toss money into a tollbooth basket, the frigid air brought her back to her senses, and she knew that Leo would see right through it. She was being naïve. No one would buy it. If she was going to clear Jim, she'd have to do it with hard evidence.

But where would she get that? She didn't have access to the kind of information that would clear a man of a serious crime. Anyway, she hadn't even seen the evidence against him. What was she going to do if she found he'd been meeting with hoodlums or passing drugs to kids in school grounds?

She scolded herself again for thinking negatively. It wasn't going to be easy, following her father's advice. She usually assumed the worst in an effort to protect herself. She didn't want to get her hopes up any more — not since Scott's life had been stolen from her.

That's the way she saw it. Someone had stolen Scott. She knew it was the enemy, the author of death, the one who comes to steal and to kill and to destroy. That supreme scoundrel had nearly ruined her life. She knew her God would be ultimately victorious and that He was still in absolute control. But she had learned a painful, bitter lesson from that loss. For as long as she was on this earth, she could take nothing for granted. She could look to a bright future, a time of consummation, an eternal home of peace. But she fought expecting too much from this present world.

That's why it took her so long to realize her true feelings about Jim. She was not only building her defences against another disappointment. She was running full speed away from her feelings. She had enjoyed Jim. She had looked forward to seeing him. She had delighted in the quiet, peaceful, unpressured moments with him.

But she had not allowed herself to even consider that she might be falling in love with him. She wasn't blind. She knew what he was thinking, though he was cautious, sensitive, biding his time.

He wasn't pushy, wasn't rushing anything. She was amazed, when she thought about it, how childlike and innocent their relationship had been for so long — especially in this day and age (as her mother always said).

Perhaps he could have expected more from her. More encouragement. More affection. More response. It was clear theirs was not a brother-sister relationship; yet it could have appeared that way.

They told life stories, told secrets, told what they liked about each other. They walked hand-in-hand for hours, yet she worked hard — maybe too hard — at giving clues that said she was not open to an embrace or a kiss.

He'd been so understanding, though they never discussed it. It was one of the things she so appreciated about him. Could he sense that it was her loss that made her want to move so slowly, not just in the physical aspect, but in the whole area of commitment?

It wasn't that he made advances and then didn't act upset when she didn't respond. No, he could read her better than that. She didn't think she had been obnoxious about it; she had simply not encouraged it. And somehow, he understood.

With Scott, the relationship was probably typical, she thought. They liked each other. Then they missed each other. They wanted to be together. They talked about it, kidded each other about it, flirted, and joked about their marriage long before they had known each other well enough to be discussing it seriously. As they grew in their love, their jokes about being man and wife evolved into serious discussions of their plans.

Jennifer didn't know what she would have done if that same progression had begun with Jim. It would have put her off, certainly. She would have seen the similarities, known where it was leading, and she would have tried to jump off the carousel.

Not that she didn't care for Jim or had any reservations about him at all. But she was going to be careful this time. She was going to be sure; she was going to be realistic; she was going to be even a little fatalistic, though she had been counselled not to be.

Both her father and her pastor had told her that she wouldn't really protect herself by locking herself in a cocoon and insuring herself against another devastating disappointment. Both felt she would do better to concentrate on the tremendous odds — morbid though it might be to consider them — against someone suffering two such painful blows in one lifetime.

'Then you're saying that since it's so unlikely that I'd be twice widowed,' she asked her pastor, 'that I should just put it out of my mind and not worry about it?'

'I'm aware how unrealistic that has to sound to someone whose wound is so fresh,' he had said. And she nodded. 'And also coming from someone who has never suffered that kind of pain.' And she nodded again, not intending to be cruel. 'But Jennifer, you can survive this thing when you are able to pull yourself up and out of it with the help of your friends and your family and your God.'

It had sounded so pompous and pietistic; and yet, as she mulled it over during the many hard months to follow, she saw the wisdom of it. She also knew the absence of anything else to say to the bereaved. The less said the better, she decided. She had learned, at least, how to best comfort grieving loved ones. You stand there, you hold their hand, you put your arm around them, you sit with them, you cry with them, you do something for them without offering or being asked, and you keep your mouth shut. Because when you say that you don't know what to say, you're proving just that. And when you think that there's nothing you can say that will change anything or assuage the grief, you are right, and your quiet actions speak so much louder than your empty words. Jennifer almost missed her exit. *What's wrong with me?* she wondered. *Am I so worried about Leo that I'm burying myself in these gloomy thoughts?* She turned on an all-news radio station to hear if there was anything that would prepare her for Leo. After a few minutes, the city's most popular topic was in the news again.

Two of the four police officers
arrested just after midnight this
morning have already been released
on bond. Originally, no bond was set
for the four, but attorneys for both
Sergeant William Much and Patrol
Officer Trudy Janus won emergency
bond concessions late this morning,
citing precedence in the previous
police shakeup during which all
charged officers had been released to
the custody of their attorneys,
pending hearings.

No bond has been set in the case of
Sixteenth Precinct Lieutenant Frank
Akeley, who has been charged with
the near fatal shooting of Internal
Affairs Division Chief John Lucas
during Akeley's arrest. Akeley's
attorney, the noted municipal
barrister, Carl Williams, has sought
no concessions for his client at this
point.

The fourth arrested officer,
specially assigned Patrol Officer
James Purcell, has still not secured
representation and has reportedly
refused the offer of a public defender.
So though bond is apparently
available for those officers who did
not resist arrest, Purcell remains in
the headquarters lockup at this hour.

There has been speculation that

Frank Akeley's high-powered attorney might enter a self-defence plea and that counsel for Sergeant Bill Much may have already made overtures toward plea bargaining by offering his client as a state's witness.

The attorney for Ms. Janus, however, has released a statement that her client will be entering an emphatic not guilty plea.

In a related humorous note, if anything about this case can be considered funny, Jake Rogers, columnist for the *Chicago Day* writing in a special midday edition, has noted the irony of Singing Policeman Bill Much offering to continue to sing about his and his colleagues roles in this latest scandal....

Jennifer had always enjoyed Jake's columns. Until today. Her personal involvement in this case made it impossible for her to see any humour in it. She wondered if she would have anyway. There was something terribly sad about whatever it was that caused people to leave their ideals and bring shame on themselves and their families and their co-workers.

She wondered what bond had been set. If it was less than $50,000, perhaps she could scrape together the 10 per cent of that necessary to get Jim out.

Jennifer parked behind the *Day* building on Michigan Avenue, wishing she'd stopped at her apartment to pick up her notes. She didn't know if Leo wanted her to work or what. But by his tone on the phone, it could have been anything from a change of his mind to a new break in the story or even a true calling on the carpet. She hadn't faced his anger since that first week under his supervision, but his tongue lashings were legendary.

She planned to stop at the washroom mirror for one last peek, but she saw Bobby Block heading down the back passageway toward her.

'Hi, Jenn! Didn't know you were going to be in today.'

'Neither did I. What's happening, Bobby?'

'In the big one? Not much. Lucas has stabilized, but the docs are still doubtful about his recovery. Still on machines and everything. The arresting officers' names are out. Everybody's got 'em. Can't imagine how long they thought they were gonna keep those quiet with all the uniformed guys they pulled in for assistance.'

'Yeah, Leo told me when he called.'

'Guess their days with Internal Affairs are just about over. You know, once all the other cops know —'

'Yes, I know.'

'Guess your time with the *Day* is just about over too, huh?'

Jennifer eyed him warily. 'What are you talking about, Bobby?'

'Leo didn't tell you a couple of them were in here today?'

'Who?'

'The arresting officers. The ones who busted that singing sergeant and the young Sunday school type. They were with Leo and the big boss more'n an hour, showing them pictures and reports and stuff, as far as I could tell. Leo didn't tell me anything, but I'm guessing they were telling Leo and Cooper about you and that cop.'

Jennifer was stunned, but chose to ignore Bobby's attack for the moment. '*Max Cooper* was in on it?' she said.

'Who'd you think I meant by big boss? Nobody around here bosses the publisher, do they?' He looked smug. After months of playing the dutiful subordinate, Bobby had sensed his opening and turned on her.

Jennifer looked at her watch. It had been an hour and forty-five minutes since she'd talked to Leo. 'Gotta run, Bobby. But thanks a lot for the loyalty and for telling Leo about me.'

He smiled condescendingly. 'I didn't have to, Jennifer. But I would have.'

She shot through the swing-doors to the newsroom and moved straight through to the city room. No one looked up from their desks, for which she was glad. She didn't want to appear rude, but she *was* late.

She unbuttoned her coat as she neared her desk and draped it on her chair on the way by, noticing several memos and a stack of mail. It hadn't seemed that long since she'd been in. Leo was at his desk in his window-enclosed office, pretending to edit copy, but she knew him too well for that.

He had seen her the minute she hit the city room, and his pencil hadn't moved since. She tried to take a few deep breaths and be ready for anything, but her anxiety caught up with her and left her huffing and puffing.

Forgetting to knock, she breezed into Leo's office with an apology for being late. 'Ran into Bobby on the way and shouldn't have stopped to talk.'

Without standing when she entered — as was his custom — Leo motioned to a chair and took off his reading glasses. He looked at her with raised brows, his chin still lowered as if he could have just as easily stayed with his work. She fell silent, deciding on the safest course, but her chest heaved as she tried to catch her breath without gasping.

Leo leaned forward and slowly pulled his day-old unlit cigar from his cheek and laid it gently in his personal ashtray, one which hadn't ever seen an ash. He picked up the tray and placed it behind him on an overhanging bookshelf, out of consideration for her, Jennifer hoped.

He turned around again to face her and leaned back in his chair, putting his feet on the desk and his hands behind his head. With his slightly frumpy academic look, sleeves rolled up and tie loosened, she couldn't help thinking what an archetypical newspaper editor he was. And how right now he was milking his authority over her for all it was worth.

She wanted to say, 'Let's get on with it, Leo. What's on your mind?' But she wouldn't dare do that with Leo Stanton. And just when she thought she'd burst if he *didn't* get on with it, he spoke.

'You were running late, but you stopped to chat to Bobby.'

'Yes, I shouldn't have. I'm sorry.'

'It's all right. At least, it's understandable. I mean, he works for you. Admires you. Looks up to you. Aspires to be like you.'

'Oh, I wouldn't say —'

'I'm not trying to flatter you, Jennifer. I'm trying to make a bigger point, because there's something about your stopping to talk to Bobby that *isn't* understandable. You know what that is?'

She shook her head.

'The fact that you would tell me that was why you were late. I'm your boss. You should try to impress me. You *do* try to impress me. And that's OK. I do the same thing with my boss. Only I do it in a different way.

'If I was late to a meeting with my boss, I'd tell him it was the traffic, or car trouble, or anything other than the truth if the truth were so lame that it made me look bad. Don't you think it made you look bad that you were late to what you have to know is a very important meeting with your boss because you lost track of the time?'

'Well, yes, that's why I told you I was sorry, and I really am. It was inexcusable, and I hope you'll forgive me.'

'If it's inexcusable, how can I forgive you?'

'Leo, I don't understand. I'm sorry. You're right. I was wrong. It won't happen again. If you want the whole truth, frankly I was gently pumping Bobby to see what would make you call me back to work from a day off.'

'*You* don't understand? *I* don't understand. You're not just so honest that you tell me the real reason you were late; you tell me *more.* I've always appreciated your honesty, Jenn. It's one of the many things I like about you.'

'Thank you, Leo, but it's not like you to beat around the bush. It's apparent you're leading up to something.'

'If you don't mind my saying so, Jennifer, it's your whole honesty kick that leaves me so disappointed in you today.'

He paused as if expecting a reaction from her. She had decided to say nothing more until he got to his point. Leo's lips tightened and he slid his feet off the desk to the floor and sat forward again.

'Jennifer, Jennifer. Why didn't you tell me about you and James Purcell?'

8 'There was nothing to tell, Leo.'

Her boss shook his head sadly and looked away from her, making her feel low. 'A police reporter fraternizing with a police officer and there was nothing to tell? Tell me we've never discussed the danger of this, Jennifer.'

'Of course we have, but the man was one of my first contacts. He was desk officer at the Sixteenth when I started. And when he was reassigned to duty that would never be something I would cover, I didn't see the harm in seeing him.'

'Do you now?'

'I guess, but —'

'You guess? Can you tell me that wasn't the reason you were crying over that article last night?'

'It was, but it didn't show in the piece, did it?'

'You shouldn't have written the article. You were biased.'

'But it didn't show.'

'You think the man is innocent.'

'And you think he's guilty, Leo. Doesn't that make you biased?'

'I have every reason to believe he's guilty. Everyone believes he's guilty. Everyone but you.'

'I hadn't planned to start seeing him, Leo. And I've never used him for information.'

'But it had to colour your view of the police, didn't it?'

'No, it didn't. It really didn't. I have no doubt that Akeley shot Lucas, and not out of self-defence. Much has all but admitted he was guilty by offering himself up as a state's witness. And Janus has been a pistol ever since she joined the force. Her involvement in this wouldn't surprise me.'

'Me either, Jenn. I agree with you all the way down the line except in one specific case: your boyfriend. Your relationship *had* to affect your view of him. They're all guilty and he's not? How do you reconcile that? Because you know him? What if you knew the others and developed a little sympathy for them? What if you'd heard Bill Much singing "The Big Brown Bear" to a bunch of school kids and knew he had a teenage daughter with braces and that he coached his boys for baseball? Then would you say, "Well, Akeley shot a man and Trudy Janus is a pistol, but my boyfriend and good ol' Bill Much, they're innocent"?'

'You don't understand,' Jennifer said quietly.

'I didn't hear you.'

'You don't understand how well I know Jim.'

'I don't? I don't think I *want* to understand how well you know him! I'm trying to work out this little game of deceit about your relationship with him and how that all fits in with your church and Sunday school thing; now don't get really honest with me and tell me you're having an affair with the man.'

'I'm not. Of course I'm not. We haven't even kissed.'

Leo almost had to suppress a smile. 'I don't want to hear all of it, Jennifer. If you church types carry on serious romantic relationships without even kissing, that's just too interesting. I'm telling you you deceived me by saying nothing about it. You should have told me the first night he picked you up from the office.'

'You would have taken me off the police beat,' she said slowly.

'Possibly.'

'That would have been unnecessary.'

'You see what's happened and you can say that? The man is the laughingstock of this town because of his fresh-scrubbed image and now being up on charges, and you tell me it isn't significant that my police reporter is a very close personal friend?'

'How do you know how close or how personal or how much of a friend? He helped me with my car one night, and we've dated a few times.'

Leo stood. 'Can't you see it's too late to try to fool me about this?'

'I've never tried to fool you!'

'No, but you don't tell me everything either, do you?'

'I didn't tell you about Jim because I was afraid you would misunderstand something that did not and is not and will not affect my work.'

'You're right that I would have misunderstood. You're wrong that it isn't or won't affect your work.'

'It didn't.'

'Granted.'

'It isn't.'

'If you'd seen yourself hunched over your VDT and bawling your eyes out last night, you wouldn't say that.'

'But Leo! The story didn't show it!'

'Granted.'

'It won't affect me in the future; I can promise that. I can be objective.'

'Wrong. You don't want to write a piece about the "real" Jim Purcell? You're not tempted to try to unload a piece on me about some of the things he's said over the past several months that prove that he just couldn't be the man everyone thinks he is?'

Jennifer was stunned. It was as if Leo had read her mind. But she *had* finally decided against that strategy. 'No,' she said weakly.

'How many times have you dated Purcell?'

'I don't know. Quite a bit.'

'How much is "quite a bit"?'

'I don't know, Leo. What are you driving at?'

'You want to know how many times you've seen him since that night your car broke down in front of the Sixteenth Precinct?'

'Did I say that's where it broke down?'

'Am I wrong? Where did it break down?'

'You're right.'

'Do you want me to tell you where you went that night and the next Saturday? And the weekend after that? And Monday evening before the arrest? You want me to tell you where you had dinner and how long you stayed there and whether he opened the door for you? You want to see pictures of yourself in the car-park with him?'

Jennifer couldn't speak.

'I don't enjoy this, Jennifer. But I think you're going to regret not telling me that you've been seeing a man on your beat.' And he sat back down, rolled his chair back to his credenza, pulled open a file drawer, and produced a manila envelope full of black and white photographs.

He spread them on the desk before him. Jim and Jennifer at Ravinia. Jim and Jennifer at the beach. At dinner. At a concert. At a sports fixture. In the car-park of her apartment building. At her church. At his church. Everywhere but at her home.

'You want pictures of you in a car with him on the Northwest Tollway?'

She shook her head. Her face was hot. 'So you had me followed. You found out about Jim, and you put a tail on me. That's low. But what do you see in your pictures? Anything out of line? Anything more than holding hands?'

Leo stood again and sat on the edge of his desk, staring down at Jennifer and slowly shaking his head. 'Jenn, you can't really think I'd do that. That's not me. I would have confronted you. I haven't the time or the money to put a tail on you. For what reason would I do that? To build some sort of a case against you? If I had known, I would have taken you off the beat, that's all. You wouldn't have been able to talk me into leaving you on. You wouldn't have been able to convince me that it could work, because it never does. It's Murphy's Law, kid. Look what happened. You wouldn't have predicted this in a million years.'

'So where'd you get the pictures, Leo?'

Leo pulled two business cards from his

pocket and read them. 'From Special Investigator Raymond Bequette and Detective Donald Reston, IAD.'

'I'll bite,' she said. 'What's it all about?'

'They'd like to talk to you.'

'About *what?*'

'About your relationship with a man who has been under surveillance and under suspicion for drug dealing for more than a year, since before he left Vice Control Division.'

'They think he sold me drugs? Or that I supplied them? Did they get any pictures of that?'

'If you'd done that, they'd had pictures, you can be sure of that.'

'Their pictures tell the whole story of our relationship. They know where we went and how long we stayed there and how many times we went out. That's more than I know. What could I tell them?'

'They don't know, but you spent as much time with him as anyone during the time he was trafficking in drugs. They think you might be able to shed a little light on the subject for them.'

'What do you think, Leo? I've told you why I didn't think our relationship was anything you needed to be aware of, and I admit I was breaking the rules, rationalizing, whatever you want to call it. I love my job, and I love working for you, and I wanted that *and* my relationship with Jim. I can see how it's got me into bigger trouble, and I'm sorry it cost you your confidence in me. But do you think that I could be aware that Jim was doing what they think he was doing and still keep seeing him? Could I have become aware of his activity and then not told you of my mistake?'

'I can't imagine.'

'Thanks for that, anyway.'

'You're welcome, but I also can't understand you're being so close to the man for this long and not catching on.'

'Catching on to what? Have you considered the possibility that I know the man better than people who shoot pictures with a telephoto lens from a hundred yards away? I'm telling you that Jim Purcell is the farthest thing from a drug dealer I've ever met. He never talked about it. He never used it. He never possessed it. He never ran in those circles. It just isn't true, Leo.'

Leo reached back into the same drawer and produced another envelope full of photographs. He scooped up the ones of Jim and Jennifer and replaced them with a couple of dozen shots of James Purcell with other people.

Jennifer put a trembling hand up to her mouth, and, as much as she wanted to pull away and run from the room, she couldn't take her eyes off the pictures. Even in dark glasses, Jim was recognizable. Even in shots taken by infrared camera in the dead of night, it was most definitely him.

There were pictures of him in broad daylight, some in uniform, some in clothes she didn't recognize, some with his hair styled differently. But it was him. He was talking to Frank Akeley at a street corner, taking something from Trudy Janus in the car-park of a shopping centre on Western Avenue, in conference with Bill Much somewhere in town, looking around to be sure no one was watching.

There he was with known hoodlums from outside the police department too. The mob-related figure from south of the Loop whom Jennifer had written a story about when he was sentenced in the spring. The gang leader from the West Side ghetto who was up on charges six times before being sent to prison a few months earlier. The police officer who was fired after being convicted of stealing truckloads of car tyres.

'You recognize some of these creeps?'

She nodded, shuddering.

'Your boyfriend got too close to the fire one too many times, and IAD got him. You want to see more?'

She didn't, but part of her needed to. She wasn't going to let this thing drop until she had talked to Jim. Love may not have been what she felt for the sad looking creature in the photos, but she did pity him. He surely wouldn't have a friend in the world once all the dirt came out.

So this was what was going to happen to

her love if she found he was guilty. It wasn't so much anger and resentment. It was pity. And wonder. And curiosity. When had it started? What caused it? What made him so good at concealing it from even the woman he appeared to love?

Why would he risk his cover by spending time with a police reporter? Did knowing that she had been fooled give him the false sense of security that allowed him to be the subject of so much surveillance without his catching on? Did it ultimately lead to his arrest? Should she take some morbid comfort in that? That she may have been partially responsible for his finally being stopped by providing him a sense of well-being that he shouldn't have had?

She had a feeling the bitterness would return — the bitterness she had felt when she first suspected him. But for now she was stunned. 'Let me see the other photos,' she said.

'The other material isn't photos. It's documents, affidavits.'

She scanned a few. Depositions taken from policemen at lower levels. Civilian drug dealers, some in prison, some still on the street, telling of their contacts within the police department. Some of it dated back many years. Much of it related to the big scandal a year and a half before.

But the parts that related to Jim Purcell went back to just before he had left VCD.

That's where it had started. Had he been sincere about his reasons for getting out? She had thought of sexual temptation, maybe financial temptation. She'd never thought of drugs, let alone dealing.

But maybe that was it. He left VCD to clean up his act, to get an assignment — he had hoped in Homicide — where drugs were irrelevant. But he got into the wrong precinct. He got in where the big stuff was going on, and he couldn't stay out.

Why was she pitying him? If he had lived a lie for all those months and — as she had told her father — thumbed his nose at her love, he didn't deserve anything from her.

'What does this all mean for me, Leo?'

'I've been thinking a lot about that, Jenn. I can see you were hoodwinked by this guy, and that makes me feel bad. I never really reckoned that you knew all this, or I'd have let you go without even talking with you. But that wouldn't have been fair. Now that I've talked to you, I have to lay it out straight.

'I'm suspending you indefinitely for insubordination for not telling me of a relationship that was potentially dangerous for the *Day*. You have no idea what it was like for me today, begging the boys from IAD not to release your name to any other media. They agreed not to, but they couldn't guarantee for how long. They want to talk to you, as I said, but there's no telling what might happen after that.

'So you're off the beat and off the job until this whole police thing is over. That could be a year. And the only way I can let you back is if your guy is acquitted or if your name *never* gets into it. Now we both know Purcell is as good as up the river. And I've got to tell you that I'd have to wait two years of not seeing your name associated with this thing anywhere before I'd be comfortable in putting you back on the beat.'

It was as if he had punched her in the stomach. He hadn't said she was actually fired, but he might as well have. What was she supposed to do for two years? Hibernate? Go to a competitor? With his sense of justice, Leo would tell anyone who called for a reference that they should be careful of her for a while.

Now what? Run home again? He had said IAD wanted to talk to her. He had also said that if he had let her go without even talking to her, it wouldn't have been fair. Was she being fair to Jim? Didn't she owe it to him, if not to herself, to talk to him before she abandoned him?

Her father had said to believe in Jim until he was proved guilty. Neither of them knew how quickly that might happen. But had he meant 'proved' guilty, or 'found' guilty by a court? Was she grasping at straws? Perhaps. But she decided she would do everything in her power to follow her father's advice, at least until she talked to Jim. IAD first, then Jim.

'I understand, Leo,' she said lifelessly. 'Are you going to be able to keep this out of the *Day*, I mean with Bobby knowing?'

'Bobby knows?'

She nodded.

'You told Bobby, but you didn't tell me?'

'*I* didn't tell him, Leo. I thought *he* told *you*!'

'He never told me anything, the little —' He caught himself. 'Ah, anyway, I'll deal with him. I'm sorry, Jenny. I'm going to miss you. I loved you like a sister. A daughter anyway.'

His calling her Jenny grated on her, and she almost asked him not to ever call her that again. But then she realized that she probably wouldn't have to worry about it.

9 Jennifer appeared upset enough as she cleaned out her desk that no one had the courage to ask what was going on. It was apparent she was leaving, and not just for a few days. They'd have to find out from Leo.

One of her messages was from Donald Reston of the IAD. It said she could locate him the next afternoon at the Numbers Racket Club on Dearborn. Jennifer was grateful that she didn't have to talk to him right away.

She went home and tried to sort things out. Jennifer knew she was tired, but she just couldn't sleep. Most of the night she sat by the window, staring into the dark — talking to herself and thinking and praying.

She realized how dog-tired she was the

next day when she stepped from her car on Dearborn. Money for this meter would not be reimbursed by the *Day*. It was a good thing Scott had left her some money. More than half of it had been spent on the funeral and the cost of settling his modest estate, but there was enough left to live on for a while if necessary. But probably not enough to last long if she used any of it to bail Jim Purcell out of jail.

I must be tired, she thought. *Still thinking about getting him out after seeing those pictures Leo has. What's the matter with me?* She decided she was so enamoured of her own father that she had been somehow catapulted into a benefit-of-the-doubt-giving posture that couldn't be shaken, even by condemning pictures and affidavits.

There was something about the whole ordeal that still didn't sit well with her, but she couldn't put her finger on it. It wasn't that she thought she was above being conned. Nor that Jim would have been incapable of it. But she thought she had glimpsed the core of the man. And what she had seen in Jim was not what she'd seen in the photographs. Oh, those were pictures of him, all right. But if she had to choose between the two personas, she'd choose the one she knew, not just because that was the way she wanted it or because that would make it all pleasant, but because she really felt — down

deep — that she knew the real Jim Purcell.
And she loved him.

Did she, could she, love him if the Jim in
the pictures was the real character? No, she
decided. She couldn't. She wouldn't be
reacting this way if she knew for sure that
he was guilty. But she didn't know if she
was reacting this way because she wasn't
convinced of his guilt, or if she wasn't convinced of his guilt because of the way she
was reacting. That would sound crazy to a
person like Don Reston. It even sounded
crazy to Jennifer.

She asked for Reston at the counter and
was directed to racquetball court number
three. She watched from the cutout in the
wall upstairs and tried to guess which
player was Reston. Not knowing the game,
it was hard for Jennifer to tell who was
winning or what was going on. But the most
agile, the most in-shape player was a tall,
almost gangly, dark-haired man in red
shorts and a blue cutoff sweatshirt. He was
playing barefoot, which she didn't understand either.

Decked out in a jogger's ensemble was an
older man, probably mid-forties, who was
paunchy, sweated a lot, and was always
stopping to catch his breath. He was an all
right player, she guessed. But the taller man
dominated. He started each play, when he
was in control of the ball, by bouncing it
very lightly on the floor so that it rose only a

few inches, and then he didn't hit it until it was on its way down again.

The taller man stepped and twisted his whole body and drove his racket into the ball with such force that it slammed off the front wall and came hurtling at the ankles of his opponent, usually causing him to dance just to get his racket on it.

Jennifer folded her coat neatly over her arm and leaned against the ledge. She watched and thought for several minutes, guessing the taller man was Reston. Suddenly the other man lost his balance while stepping into a low shot close to the front wall. As she watched him tumble to the floor, she nearly missed seeing the ball careen off the wall and head straight at her. As she dropped out of sight, she saw the tall man whirl to follow the flight of the ball.

'A little help, please,' he called.

She ran after the ball and retrieved it just before it would have bounced down the carpeted stairway. Embarrassed, she tossed it through the opening again without showing her face. But when she didn't hear the game begin again, she cautiously peered down.

Both men were looking at her. They smiled and looked at each other. 'It's her,' the older one said.

'Jennifer Grey?' asked the younger.

She nodded.

'Can you give me a minute to polish off this game, and we'll be right with you?'

She'd been right. It was Reston. When they'd finished, he hollered back up at her. 'We'll grab a shower, then we can talk right here, if that's all right with you.'

They looked both tired and refreshed later in casual clothes as they sat across from her in overstuffed chairs in the upstairs lounge. She found herself strangely nervous, though she'd interviewed cops hundreds of times.

'I'm Don Reston; call me Don. This is Ray Bequette; call him Gramps.' The men laughed. Jennifer tried to.

'Let's get right to the point, Miss Grey.'

'Mrs.'

'Oh, I'm sorry. I guess we just thought —'

'You thought that since I'm dating, I couldn't be a widow.'

'I'm sorry, ma'am; I was unaware of that. Your boss told you by now, no doubt, that the Internal Affairs Division has been observing you and Officer Purcell for many months. Were you totally unaware of his involvement in the drug scene?'

'I still am.'

'I beg your pardon?'

'I still am totally unaware of his involvement in the drug scene.'

'I was under the impression that Mr. Stanton was to show you some of the results of our surveillance.'

'I saw your photographs and your affidavits.'

'Then you can't really say you are completely in the dark about our suspicions of Purcell.'

'Fair enough. I know what you think about him, and I know what people have said about him. But I never had an inkling about this, and I'm not ready to accept it.'

'What more will it take to convince you?'

'I need to talk to him, of course.'

'We can arrange that.'

'You can?'

'Certainly.'

'What's in it for you?'

'We need a little information. We thought you might be willing to help us get it.'

'You mean trying to get something out of him that I would then pass along to you? You've got to be kidding. I couldn't do that.'

'You're above that?'

'I'm not an undercover cop. Maybe if I were I'd throw my scruples to the wind.'

'Your boss told us he thought you were in the dark about Purcell until now too.'

'He was right. Can you tell me something? How much of your information did you get from my assistant at the *Day?*'

The two looked at each other. 'I didn't even know you had an assistant until I heard from your boss. Stanton called this morning and told me that he had reprimanded your assistant because he knew about you and Purcell and never said a word to Stanton about it. Stanton reckoned he was trying to set you up so he could have your job.'

Jennifer sat back and stared at the wall.

'Do you mind if we get back to your boyfriend?'

'You mean back to the dirty work you just asked me to do?'

'Purcell betrayed you.'

'Possibly.'

'You wouldn't like to return the favour?'

Jennifer removed her coat from her lap and draped it on a nearby chair. She looked first at Reston, then at Bequette. 'Maybe if I really thought he was guilty, I could justify this.'

'How are you going to find out?'

'I'm going to ask him. To the best of my knowledge, he has never lied to me. He's answered everything I've ever asked him. I know him well, I think. If he's trying to fool me, I'll know when I ask him straight out.'

'And if you determine that he is what we think he is?'

'I'll be disappointed, of course.'

'Of course. But will you tell us what he says?'

'I'll think about it.'

'We can only arrange a meeting for you if you agree to give us information afterward.'

'And what if I become convinced during our conversation that he is innocent?'

Reston and Bequette looked at each other. Reston shrugged. Bequette took over in a fatherly manner. 'Mrs. Grey, I hate to tell you, but apparently you're not getting our drift. The man is guilty. There is no doubt about that. We have enough evidence to put him away for years. We don't want information from you that will incriminate him. We simply want all we can get from him in the event that he doesn't turn state's witness. Frankly, this move of his not to seek counsel was a crafty thing to do, and it makes us nervous. Whatever he was trying to accomplish with it, it worked. We don't know what he's up to, but apparently he's stalling for some reason.

'It could be he's worried about some of his key contacts, worried that they'll try to harm him now that he's been burned. That's a good reason to stay in jail. Maybe someone else is clearing out of town while he's stalling us. This is our last case with IAD, and we'd like to clean the thing up right, wouldn't you?'

'I have no problem with what you're trying to do. It's just that I would have to be totally convinced that Jim's guilty before I could ever cooperate with you in trying to implicate other people by getting information out of him.'

Bequette turned to Reston and talked quietly, though not trying to keep Jennifer from hearing. 'Don, I frankly don't think the man will try to maintain his innocence any longer. He hasn't announced how he'll plead, but he's got to know what we've got on him. If she goes in there under the assumption that he's guilty and that the sham is over, my guess is he'd give it up and would try to determine if Mrs. Grey here would stick by him or throw him over. If he does that — and we might be able to help that happen by getting him special permission to talk to her longer in a more casual setting than the interview cells — then she'll know, and, if I'm reading her right, she'll help us out all she can.'

Reston looked to Jennifer. She tilted her head and pursed her lips as if to say, 'I suppose.' What she did say was, 'Well, if Jim *tells* me he's guilty, I can't argue with that, can I?'

'I don't see how he can say otherwise,' Bequette said. 'I've been concentrating on Bill Much for several months, but of course I've helped Don tail Purcell at times too. We've all worked together on this case, each specializing on one of the four and helping out with the others.'

'Jim was your mark?' Jennifer asked Reston.

'Yes, ma'am. I'd been seeing a lot of you two together lately.'

'Yeah, well, I'm not too thrilled about that. But tell me, what did you see Jim do?'

'With you?'

'No, I know that. What your camera saw was all there was to see.'

'That's what we thought. You never spent time with him at his place or yours, did you?'

'I've never even been *in* his place.'

Reston shook his head in wonder. 'So anyway, you were asking?'

'What you saw Jim do while you were tailing him all this time. I didn't see your name in the affidavits, did I?'

'No, my deposition and testimony will come nearer the time of the trials. It takes us weeks to prepare our presentations, and of course, each of us will talk about what we saw all four suspects doing.'

'And what I give you — if I do — from my talk with Jim — will go into your testimony?'

'Absolutely.'

'Then I'd better be sure he's guilty. And that he wilfully betrayed me. And that I'm up to this kind of revenge.'

'I don't think you should call it revenge,' Reston said. 'It's the civic duty of any law-abiding citizen.'

'That's a little idealistic after what I've been through with Jim the past several months,' she said.

'I've been through a few things with him too,' Reston said.

'Are you going to give me some examples?'

'What do you want to hear?'

Jennifer was growing impatient. 'Anything. Something solid. Something incriminating. Something that will convince me the way you're convinced.'

Reston stood and walked to the iron railing that overlooked the ground floor. Joggers were padding past. He put both hands on the rail and hung his head low to his chest. He turned and came back, sitting right next to Jennifer, which startled her. His dark eyes looked weary.

'Let me tell you something,' he said. 'I don't much like the job I've had to do the last couple of years. I don't like spying on cops, even bad ones. I don't get any big kick out of building a case against someone and knowing it's going to ruin him for ever. I know these guys deserve it, and I know that ruining them for life is the price we pay to get them off the street — and getting them off the street is something I have no qualms about because we deal with the results of drug addiction in nearly every case we handle, week in and week out.

'And when that surveillance work is over, like it is now, the toughest part of the process begins. We take our notes and our photos and our tape recordings, and we start a written case against someone, a case that is so airtight that we never have to worry that our work has been in vain.

'I could sit here and tell you stories about James Purcell that would take me all night. Places I've seen him, people I've seen him with, marked money I've seen him take, drugs I've checked in that he's sold to undercover narcs. You want just one incident? I wouldn't know where to start.

'There's something we don't do, Mrs. Grey. We don't arrest them and then see them on the street again. When IAD has busted a guy, he stays busted. Because we wouldn't even go to the trouble of the dangerous arrest of an armed man unless we had him so dead to rights that we didn't have to worry that he was going to get away with something.

'My boss, one of the best in the business, is probably never going to wake up again, never see his wife and his daughters again, never be a great example to young cops again because your boyfriend's boss tried to kill him. A cop shot a cop, and don't let anybody ever tell you that Frank Akeley didn't know who he was firing on Tuesday morning.'

Reston had grown emotional, and Bequette looked concerned. Jennifer's last vestiges of hope were fleeting. He sounded so sure. He ought to be sure. He *was* sure.

'I put the responsibility for the shooting of John Lucas right in the laps of every one of the big four in the Sixteenth Precinct. Every one of 'em ought to get the chair if he dies, because they all had a hand in it. They were the reason he was on the street that night, doing a job that a lesser boss wouldn't have done.

'So you see why I don't want to talk about the specifics in the James Purcell case? You see why these guys, all of them, make me sick when I think about them? You'll get your specifics. They'll all come out in the trial, and they'll be in every paper in town.'

Jennifer was sorry she had asked. She couldn't speak, but she tried to tell him with her expression that she at least understood what he was trying to say.

Bequette broke the tension. 'You still want to see Purcell?'

She nodded.

'All right. We'll set it up. You'll get a call. Probably from Purcell himself; he hasn't used his call yet. And you'll be able to talk to him in the anteroom downtown. You'll be searched and will be allowed to take nothing in or out with you. But we'll give you all the time you need.'

'When?'

'Tomorrow morning at nine.'

10 The next morning Jennifer dressed as if she were going on the most important date of her life. She was, of course. But the mirror told the story of the night before. She had been in bed twelve hours, yet she did more praying than sleeping, more thinking than dreaming.

She tried covering the dark circles under her eyes with makeup, but that backfired. She decided she looked like a raccoon and hoped that Jim would think her clothes were so nice he wouldn't notice her face.

Why am I thinking about trivia anyway? she chided herself. *How I look will be the last thing on his mind, and on mine if I can keep my thoughts straight.*

She had settled it, she decided in her car.

If Jim was guilty — and she would know either by his not trying to hide it any more or by seeing through him if he did — she felt no responsibility for his actions or for protecting him. She would lose whatever it was she felt for him, and she would feel no compulsion to keep from IAD anything he might say incriminating anyone else.

It was when she reached police headquarters downtown that she realized she had never received a confirming call — not from Jim, not from IAD, not from anyone. Should she wait until she saw Bequette or Reston? Or should she just go in and see if she was expected? There were plenty of unmarked squad cars, but how would she know if any of them belonged to men from IAD?

'I would like to see a prisoner,' she told the sergeant at the desk.

'Name?'

'Officer James Purcell.'

'No! *Your* name!'

'Jennifer Grey.'

'Press is not allowed to see prisoners, especially that one.'

'I'm not here as press, Sergeant. I have been cleared to talk to Officer Purcell.'

'You got papers?'

'No, I assumed you would have received something.'

'I got nothing.'

'Well, could you please check? It was cleared through IAD and —'

'IAD don't cut any ice around here, lady. I run the jail.'

'But wouldn't you have clearance papers for certain visitors?'

'Lemme look,' he said, disgusted. He rummaged around on his desk and came up with a yellow carbon copy of something. 'Well, whadya know?' She edged closer. 'You're to see Purcell at nine o'clock in the anteroom. It's all set.'

'Thank you.'

'Except —'

'Except?'

'Except it ain't nine o'clock yet, is it? I got to make sure I got personnel that'll allow you to be in the anteroom.'

'I was told there would be no one else in there but us.'

'Yeah, so I gotta have men outside the windows and outside the door, don't I?'

'How long will that take? It's ten to nine.'

'I don't know. I'll let you know when the room and the prisoner are ready for you, Miss Grey.'

'Mrs.'

'Whatever.'

Jennifer sat on a wooden bench for nearly forty minutes, doing everything in her power to avoid asking what was taking so long. Every time she would come to the end of her patience and start to move toward the sergeant again, he would hold up a hand and mouth silently, 'I will let you know.'

Crazy ideas floated through her head. Jim was a drug addict. A schizophrenic. He would cry and beg her to forgive him. He would deny it, but she would see through him. He had been moved. He had finally hired a lawyer and was out on bail. He had tried to escape. He had been caught. He had escaped.

'Miss Grey!'

'*Mrs.,*' Jennifer thought as she jumped up and ran over to the sergeant, but she said nothing.

'The prisoner has declined the conference,' the man said.

'What?'

'He don't wanna see anybody.'

'Does he know who's here to see him?'

'Yes, ma'am, if you want it like that, he don't wanna see you.'

Jennifer spun in a circle, confused. What was she supposed to make of this? Didn't he realize that until he got a lawyer, she was probably the only friend he had? She had held out hope — she still did — and she shouldn't have after all she'd heard. Something was still unresolved. Something he didn't know but should have. He needed to know that she loved him. That was really why she was here. Guilty or not, a future for them or not, whether she loved him when she knew the whole truth or not, he needed to know that she loved the man she knew. She had to tell him.

She hadn't been gone from her job long enough to lose her ingenuity. 'Can you get a message to him?'

'I could if I wanted to. I tol' ya — I run the jail. But I don't wanna. Bye-bye.'

'Maybe this message is as much for you as it is for him then. How would you like me to make a scene, right here in the lobby? How would you like it to appear in every paper in town that the former police reporter for the *Chicago Day* couldn't get in to see a prisoner and that she caused such a ruckus she had to be thrown out?'

'That I don't need. I'm in enough trouble as it is with all the baloney that goes on *inside* the bars. That'd be great; a fruitcake *outside* the bars goes nuts.'

'That's what you're going to have to answer for.'

'Awright, what's the message?'

'Just that. I'll make a scene that'll embarrass him and you if he won't see me.'

'He'll see ya. Wait in the anteroom.'

Jennifer couldn't believe herself. *I've gone from a half intelligent police reporter to a conniving, unemployed, boisterous, lovesick woman in two days!*

She sat at the end of a long grey table, wondering what she should do when he entered. Embrace him? Smile at him? Tear into him verbally? The door opened, and a matron came in. Jennifer was searched, and her handbag and coat and jewellery were taken. She sat back down but hadn't even had time to collect herself when Jim walked in. Her heart raced. She stood, but he sat at the other end of the table. She felt foolish standing there and sat back down.

He looked like his old self except that he was wearing city-issue blue denims. He still had that shy look, that gentle air. She didn't know what she had expected. A monster? A shouter? A hard-looking criminal?

'How are you?' she said, her voice quavering.

He ignored the question. 'I'm sorry I said I didn't want to see you, Jennifer. But it's just that the timing isn't right. I didn't want you to see me in here like this. I know you've been around these places, but you don't like seeing me in this get-up, do you?'

'That's not the reason you didn't want to see me,' she tried weakly, fighting tears. 'If I didn't see you here, where was I ever going to see you?'

'You could have seen me later. Soon.'

'Where?'

'Jennifer, the truth is there's something going on here that you know nothing about. I never told you anything about it because I simply couldn't. You don't understand it, and you won't be able to understand it until I'm able to tell you all about it.'

'I'm afraid I *do* know about it, Jim. I know more than I want to know. I can't believe you could have kept it from me all this time. I feel so stupid, so used. Betrayed.'

'But you understand why I couldn't talk about it, don't you?'

'No! Did you think I wouldn't understand?'

'Would you have?'

She bit her lip and stood, walking to the window where she saw three uniformed guards chatting. 'I don't understand how you could do this to me.'

'Jenn, there was no other way. If I had told you, it would have spoiled everything. I couldn't take the chance.'

'You don't think everything's spoiled now?'

'All we have right now is a timing problem, Jennifer.'

'You think time will heal *this* wound?'

'Jennifer, I'm gratified to hear that you miss me, and I miss you too, but this is temporary, and —'

'It goes much deeper than missing you, Jim. I love you. I need you. And now I'm so disappointed in you that I don't know what to think.'

Jim stared at her, his eyes narrowing. She pressed her lips together to keep from crying. 'There, you see?' she said, scolding him. 'I love you in spite of this, and I had decided not to!'

He stood and moved toward her, but she turned her back to him. 'Jennifer. You're disappointed in me? You love me in spite of this? In spite of what?'

'What have we just been talking about Jim? I know all about it! I've seen the pictures! I've read the reports! I've talked with the people from IAD! What are you going to do, deny it all now? What have you been saying about my not understanding what you couldn't tell me, if you're claiming now that you don't see what's come between us?'

He turned and rested both palms on the table, leaning over from the waist. Then he stood up and drew his palms to his face and slid them slowly down his cheeks. He let out a short sigh of surprise and whispered, 'You believe I've really been busted!'

Jennifer was speechless. Her mouth fell open, and she just turned to stare at him. He looked at her without turning his head and grinned. 'Jennifer! You don't really think — no, you — oh, Jenn, I'm sorry. You couldn't have thought —'

'Jim, what are you saying?'

'You said you talked to the guys at IAD? Who'd you talk to?'

'Don Reston and Ray somebody.'

'Bequette?'

'Yes.'

'And they didn't tell you?'

'They told me everything, Jim, and you're in a lot of trouble.'

'They're not telling you the truth because you're a reporter,' he guessed, but his smile

131

had frozen. He'd lost his edge, his confidence. Jennifer read the worst into it.

'I'm not a reporter any more, Jim. I lost my job because of you. And it would be worth it if I knew it had all been a big mistake.'

'You lost your job? Well, it was no mistake, Jenn. But I'm not supposed to tell you about it yet, that's all. Someone will be bailing me out soon — in fact they should have already — and then the whole story will come out.'

Jennifer sat down. 'Jim, if you're trying to tell me that you were in on this from IAD's side, I've got to tell you, I don't believe it. I don't know who's trying to con who, but they showed me some stuff that makes you look pretty bad.'

Jim's confusion and fear showed. 'Why would they show you that stuff? Did they know you'd lost your job?'

'They wanted me to pump you for information on other people who might be incriminated in the case. They showed the stuff to my boss too, and to the publisher.'

'What for, Jenn? What's it all about?'

'They thought I would know all about your drug dealing because I'd spent so much time with you the past several months. Jim, what is going on?'

'I'm not sure. I'll feel like a fool if I'm supposed to be going along with this and then I tell you everything at the drop of a hat. Maybe it's a test. Maybe I shouldn't have told you anything, but just played along, pretended I'd been caught. But I can't do that to you, Jenn. I never thought you'd really think I'd been busted. But since you did, I probably should have let you go on thinking it until this thing blew over.'

'If you think this thing is going to blow over, you'd better talk to Don Reston. He was nearly in tears today, telling me that he holds you and Much and Janus every bit as responsible for Lucas's death as Akeley.'

'Lucas died?' Jim said, almost shouting.

'No, I didn't mean that; he was saying *if* Lucas died.'

'Reston's a good actor. Could he have been bluffing?'

'For what reason? Anyway, I don't think so. He'd have had to be a better con man than you are.'

'Jenn, I want to tell you the whole story, but I have to make sure I'm not messing up the operation. We've been on this one for too long.'

'You lost me a long time ago.'

'You never told me you loved me before.'

'Jim, how can you change the subject like that?'

'I love you, too, you know.'

'Don't do this to me, Jim. I can't make it compute.'

'I couldn't tell you I loved you before because I knew we were being watched and photographed, and I didn't want you to be embarrassed by anything we did.'

'You *knew* we were being photographed? And you knew by whom?'

'Of course.'

'I've got to tell you something, Jim. If you think you have friends in IAD, you don't. Either those men I talked to today think you're as guilty as you look, or I am the worst judge of character who ever walked the earth.'

'You're serious.'

'You bet I am.'

'All right, Jennifer. I'm going to tell you what's been going on, but you can't tell anyone. If you love me, you'll protect my confidence.'

'Jim, don't do that to me, please! I've got all this evidence on one side showing that you've been living a lie in front of me for months, and I've got you on the other, telling me not to tell the people who sent me here that you told me anything. I came here under the condition that I would tell them what you said. You think you're breaking confidences; how do you like that one?'

'I don't know what to think, Jenn, but you're going to have to hear me out on this. I may be the worst undercover cop Chicago's ever had, but I don't know what else to do with a woman who says she loves me.'

Jennifer hid her face in her hands. She wanted whatever she was about to hear to be true. She raised her head and looked Jim full in the face as if to say, 'I'm listening. Pour it out.'

11 'When I first requested a transfer from Vice Control Division, I got in hot water from my captain.'

'Why did you want to transfer?'

'I already told you that, Jenn. I may have kept a lot from you, but I never lied to you, OK?'

'OK, so you left VCD because you had a hard time reconciling it with your faith.'

'Exactly. And I took a lot of heat for that inside the department, especially from my boss and his boss. They sent memos around, even up to the commissioner, trying to head off this precedent of people deciding they didn't like their assignments and all that.'

'Yes, and it was in all the papers.'

'Right, but that was by design.'

'Meaning?'

'It was staged, planned, set up. You know, Jenn, that you never got anything the police department didn't want you to have, and you never missed something they wanted you to cover. You may not have run with what they gave you, but they tried anyway.'

'I don't follow.'

'They're news manipulators. And they're good at it. I know from having spent enough time with you that you would not agree with tactics like that, but I think in some instances they have their place. It's debatable. That's why I thought Bequette and Reston were setting you up. But if they went to your boss and higher and showed them all the stuff, well I may have a serious problem — one that depends a lot on the health of John Lucas.'

'You think they could indict all of you in connection with his death?'

'No, you're still not getting it, are you?'

'No, but I'm trying. Keep going.'

'Anyway, the word inside the department was that I was some kind of a goody-goody, and there was a lot of speculation about whether they'd make a scapegoat of me so other guys wouldn't try the same thing with their assignments. Of course, most of them *want* Vice Control duty. They get a charge out of it.

'Well, right about that time, I got contacted by John Lucas. He said he liked my attitude and that he had got permission to consider me for IAD. He wanted to do some checking and interview me for several days. We met at various places and talked for hours. The one thing he told me never to forget was that a good internal affairs man has to keep secrets even from himself.'

'What did he mean by that?'

'It was an exaggeration to make a point. Most people can't keep a secret for half a day. Internal Affairs tests their guys all the time, starting rumours and seeing where they lead, how long it takes the story to get distorted and come back, and all that. Confidentiality was a major prerequisite. But it wasn't as important as an unimpeachable record.

'Lucas had checked me out and decided I was the type of person he wanted in IAD. He set it up with the commissioner for me to appear to suffer for my request of a change of assignment, and people within and without the department bought it. The people in the Sixteenth thought they were really getting me and doing the commissioner a favour by giving me the dog assignments, the night desk and then the Officer Friendly thing. It couldn't have been more perfect for what I was really assigned to do.

'Lucas gave me a couple of drug-related assignments in VCD before I was transferred. He gave me the drugs and the money, and he had his men check me out.

He was pleased when they reported back that I was somebody they could nail and that they should keep an eye on me.

'My point is this, Jennifer. For the past year or so, I have ultimately reported to John Lucas. We hardly ever saw each other because he had not even told his own men. And he trained them to stay on my tail. That made it nearly impossible for me to ever meet with him.'

'When was he going to tell his men?'

'He wasn't sure. He said he thought he might not tell them until the night of the big four arrests. You know, when Reston busted me that night, I only played along for the sake of the uniformed men with him. But I wondered if he had been told yet because he played it so straight. No winks, no jokes, no anything.'

'Well, Jim, someone else had to know. Even if Lucas decided not to tell anyone until after you were in jail, his secretary had to know, didn't she? And who checked you out for him in the first place?'

'That was just it. He did most of the checking himself, and then he assigned the ones who had checked me out first to tail me a while. After the first few drug sales in VCD, they were all convinced I was bad. Lucas told me he was getting a real kick out of having his own inside guy that no one else knew about. He didn't think it was too dangerous because it was only temporary, and his real reason was to give him a fail-safe look at his own team. They did well.'

'They did too well, Jim. But the commissioner knows, right?'

'The commissioner *should* know. Lucas reports directly and confidentially to him. Has to. That's the only way Internal Affairs can work.'

Jennifer leaned back in her chair and studied James Purcell's eyes. 'An undercover undercover undercover man. If I didn't want to believe it so badly, I probably wouldn't.'

He smiled. 'Lucas called me that once, not in those words. Said I was his triple threat. When the undercover guys investigating the undercover guys are not worthy, he's got one more ace up his sleeve.'

'Jim, do you think Bequette and Reston were having me on today and that they really know?'

'If I thought that, I'd have played along with *them.* Sorry to have to tell you that, but it has been my job for more than a year. Their talking to you and your boss and everybody and costing you your job, that's what scares me. Reston becoming emotional is nothing new. He's sincere, but he can playact that bit as well as anyone I've ever seen.'

'What do we do about them?'

'I don't worry about them unless something happens to Lucas.'

'Something could have already happened to Lucas, Jim. He's that bad.'

Purcell stood and paced. 'You want to help?'

'Why do you think I'm here?'

'To help the people who think I'm guilty, isn't that what you said?'

'I was confused. Of course I want to help. I believe you, Jim.'

He stepped behind where she sat and put his hands on her shoulders. 'That's the second-nicest thing you've said to me today,' he said. 'Anyway, I think you'd better get to Lucas's secretary and Eric O'Neill, he's the one who busted —'

'Janus. I know. I covered this story, remember?'

'Hey, if you clear me, will you get your job back?'

'I guess so. Somehow that seems insignificant right now. Anyway, I'll go and see anyone you say. Who else?'

'Well, you *could* talk to the commissioner, but let's save him as a last resort. If you don't get anywhere with the guys from IAD, send Reston and Bequette to see me. I'll see what I can do. Maybe there's something I can tell them about Lucas, some inside joke, some special name he has for them, something that will convince them that I work for the man too.'

Jennifer smiled for the first time since she had chatted with her father. 'It's nice to have a job to do,' she said. 'I'm sorry I doubted you, Jim, but it was all so —'

'I know. Listen, you were looking at dirt dug up by the Chicago PD IAD, and they're the best in the business. If I saw all they had on me, I might doubt me too. Listen, Jenn, if you don't mind, find out what you can as soon as you can, because if these guys are serious and Lucas doesn't pull through, I might as well be guilty, because I won't have a chance.'

'I'll do everything I can; you know I will. I'll be praying for you.'

'You know who *I'll* be praying for?'

'Who?'

'Lucas.'

Jennifer stood and found herself face to face with Jim Purcell, the man she realized she would have loved in spite of herself, in spite of himself, and in the middle of the most confusing time of her life. They held each other for several minutes, her face buried in his shoulder. And she cried.

Perhaps she had not done as well as her father might have hoped in her attempt to give Jim the benefit of the doubt. But now there was no longer any doubt, and she could think of no greater joy.

She drove to her apartment and bounded up the steps, wanting to laugh and cry and sing and scream all at the same time. She was reminded of her seventh birthday when her father gave her her first bicycle. He had sent her to the garage on an errand, and she had seen that beautiful bike with a big blue bow and a card with her name on it, and she ran back in tears to thank him before she even touched it. What a gift that had been. And what a gift this had been.

When she lost Scott, there was no bringing him back. She prayed that it had all been a bad dream, but it wasn't, and she knew it would always hurt. But now she had Jim. She would not let this love be snatched away, not if she had anything to say about it. And the beauty was, she had everything to say about it.

She called Don Reston and asked him to meet her as soon as possible. They met at a coffee shop on LaSalle Drive. She happily, earnestly spilled the story. 'So if you were trying to get to me through him for some reason, it didn't work because it scared him. You can be straight with me now if you know that he's working with IAD too.'

Reston stared at her sullenly. 'I'm sorry, Mrs. Grey, but I think you're a victim of a vivid imagination.'

'I'm not imagining anything. I talked to him, just like you said, and —'

'I'm talking about *his* imagination,' Reston said. 'It's just not true. Lucas would have told us, and believe me, he didn't.'

'Would anyone else in IAD know?'

'I'll call Bequette, but I'm afraid you're in

for a big disappointment. I'm not happy that you blew our assignment either, because if you had just told him you knew he was guilty —'

'I *did!* But he told me everything.'

Reston shook his head sadly. 'This is no game, ma'am. I'd have no reason to continue any ruse if what you were saying was true. But it's not. Let me call Ray.'

He slid out of the bench seat, and she called after him, 'See if you can get ahold of Mr. O'Neill for me too. Someone had to know about this.'

He nodded and was on the phone for several minutes. Jennifer looked at her watch, wondering if she could squeeze in a meeting with John Lucas's secretary before she left for lunch. She was nervous. Her foot tapped, fingers on both hands drummed the table, her eyes darted all around the coffee shop. She was on a mission she had planned to enjoy, but she didn't need any more negative reactions.

Reston returned. He looked glum. 'Listen,' Jennifer said, 'why don't you and Bequette visit Jim and talk to him yourselves?'

'We'd never get permission for something like that. It could spoil everything we're preparing for the trial. I'd really like Purcell's story to be true, for your sake. But I saw what I saw. I suppose it's possible that James Purcell was doing that stuff as part of a bigger setup. But I'm afraid unless John Lucas himself says so, I'd never be able to even admit the longshot possibility of it to anybody but you.'

'What did Mr. Bequette say?'

'His reaction was the same as mine. I tried to hit him with it before betraying my own feelings on it, just to be fair to you. He says he heard rumours years ago that Lucas liked to do this sort of thing once in a great while, but never for this long or with stakes this high. You can forget about meeting with O'Neill too. He was with Bequette. You don't want to know what *he* thought of your idea.'

'Yes I do.'

'He called it a million-to-one shot.'

Jennifer accepted the odds and headed to John Lucas's office where she waited until noon to see Gladys Balderson, the chief's secretary. She was a fussy, precise little woman — friendly, yet formal.

'No, Mrs. Grey,' she said sweetly. 'I never heard Mr. Lucas mention the name Purcell. But then much of his affairs were private, even from me. He has a file that I do not have a key to, but that is always locked away and has, in fact, in light of the shooting, been impounded.'

'How would I gain access to it? It must have Jim's name in it somewhere, even if only his initials in a meeting schedule or something. Surely Mr. Lucas couldn't have kept all his clandestine meetings in his head.'

'Surely you don't know Mr. Lucas. I would have thought you might have run into him in your work.'

'I've never talked to the man.'

'I'm sorry, you asked about access to his private file. I believe only a municipal judge or the commissioner of police could grant that, and I would find it highly unlikely in the light of your occupation.'

Jennifer didn't bother setting her straight about her current employment situation. She was running out of options. 'I know it's a long shot,' she said, 'but I wouldn't forgive myself if I didn't at least try the commissioner. Could I impose on what must be your close relationship with his secretary, your both being at the executive secretarial level and all that, and see if you can get me in to see him just for a moment this afternoon?'

'What would you want him to do, Dear, open the file for you? I'm sure he wouldn't. Probably couldn't.'

'Perhaps he could look for me. I wouldn't have to see anything. I'd just like to see if there's anything at all in that file that would indicate that Mr. Lucas was working with Jim.'

'Well, it's a possibility,' Miss Balderson said. 'I'll call Joan and see.' While dialling, she said, 'Did you hear that Mr. Lucas rallied this morning?'

'No! Really? Tell me!'

'He apparently gained consciousness early this morning, and the doctors asked the family to join him. One moment.'

While Lucas's secretary was talking to the commissioner's secretary, Jennifer prayed that God would spare the man's life. Even as she prayed it, she knew it was selfish. She couldn't care as much for a man she had never spoken with as she did about Jim, whom she loved.

'Tell me your man's full name again, Dear,' Miss Balderson said, holding a hand over the mouthpiece.

'Officer James Purcell.'

When Gladys hung up she said, 'You're in luck. The commissioner's secretary took all the information and will check it out herself. She is recording the contents of the entire file verbatim, and if she sees his initials or his name or anything remotely connected with him, if the commissioner approves, she will let you know this afternoon when you arrive for your appointment. Three o'clock. She even remembered that he is Officer Friendly, and she will look up his badge number to see if Mr. Lucas referred to him by that.'

'Oh, that's too kind,' Jennifer said.

'I don't mind telling you I'm jealous.'

'I'm sorry?'

'The man's secret file ought to be handled by his own secretary, wouldn't you think?'

12 Police Commissioner Joseph Masek appeared ill at ease with Jennifer. He began the conversation with a scowl. 'You're with the *Day*, aren't you?'

Jennifer spent several minutes explaining why she was no longer with the *Day*. 'I see,' he said slowly, pressing his fingertips together and staring at her as he leaned back in his chair.

'I can understand your concern,' he said. 'Yes, I *do* remember the request from Chief Lucas to investigate the young man who wanted to get out of Vice Control Division. I believe he thought Purcell would be the kind of guy who might make it in IAD. Frankly, my fear at the time, and I expressed it forcefully to John, was that I thought

Purcell might look *too* much like an IAD candidate. He had that fresh-scrubbed look, you know — well, of course you know, don't you? Regardless, John felt he would like to check the man out and then bring him in very gradually, test him a little, that sort of thing. I approved that, but then, of course, I removed myself from the situation.'

'You removed yourself?'

'Yes. I'm very keen to let the individual chiefs run their respective areas. Of course, in this case, John was requesting permission to manoeuvre between departments, so he came to me. Now, as a rule, all of John's activity is interdepartmental, and he doesn't need permission when he is investigating any untoward conduct, even within this office.'

'Your office?'

'Absolutely. It's the only way an IAD can work properly. He has my full backing and cooperation, and unless he's looking for personnel from another branch, he doesn't get any input from me.'

Jennifer took a deep breath. 'Well, sir, I just want to assure you that the only reason I'm here is because I'm convinced a huge misunderstanding has occurred, and I didn't know where else to turn.'

Commissioner Masek appeared sombre. 'Mrs. Grey, Officer Purcell is a close personal friend of yours, am I right?'

'Yes.'

'I have to tell you that what you have described, John Lucas using a man under-cover *within* IAD, is so highly improbable and unusual — though a very, very interesting idea — that I would have to doubt even its remotest possibility.'

'Of course it's unusual,' Jennifer pleaded, 'but that was the only way it could work. Once it comes out, it probably would never work again.'

'The point is, I really don't think John would work that way, and he and I go back many, many years. He's been a friend since the early nineteen fifties.'

'I didn't know that. You must be very worried.'

'I am indeed. My wife and I have been with Sylvia, John's wife, and two or three of the daughters off and on at the hospital ever since Tuesday morning. It doesn't look good.'

'But I understood he had rallied this morning.'

'Well, he gained consciousness for the first time since the shooting, but by the time I arrived there, he was sleeping again. Whether he had lapsed into a coma again, I don't know. But the doctor confided that not a great deal of optimism was justified. John's vital signs are still very weak, very bad.'

'May I ask another —'

'I don't hesitate to say,' the commissioner

continued, staring past Jennifer, 'that I am sick in my heart that one police officer would fire on another. It goes much deeper than just the shooting, though, Mrs. Grey. If a younger officer had done it, it might even be easier to take. Then I could say that they don't make cops like they did in my day. But Lucas and I are close to the same age, and Frank Akeley is even older. How does this happen? How does a man with a fine record get mixed up in things like this?'

Jennifer felt sudden compassion for Masek. He was lost in his grief and his fear for the life of his friend. She knew she'd feel the same for Lucas if she spent any time with him. But Lucas was almost an enemy at this point. She constantly pleaded with God to spare his life, knowing all the while that her motive was not as pure as it could be.

She wanted to feel for the man and his wife and his family, but she was thinking of Jim. She admitted silently that she was thinking of herself. Rescuing Jim from this nightmare meant new life for her too.

Commissioner Masek had asked a question to which there was no answer. But he had also interrupted Jennifer's, and she wanted to get back to it.

'Could I ask you a hypothetical question, Commissioner?'

He nodded, still staring past her.

'If John Lucas were to try something innovative as Jim, as Officer Purcell, has suggested, would you have known about it?'

'Not necessarily, no.'

'Would it have been likely that you would know?'

'No, I suppose not.'

'Then the fact that it sounds so unique to you doesn't really rule out the possibility of it.'

He squinted at her. 'Are you asking me or telling me?'

'Asking, and I'm sorry if it sounded otherwise.'

'That's all right,' he said slowly. 'Let me tell you something, may I?'

'Please.'

'I, uh, have been quite aware of you for some time.'

'You have?'

He ignored her. 'I am always very interested when a major newspaper puts a new reporter on the police beat. I frankly wasn't sure what I thought of a woman handling the job. That's not to betray any feeling I may or may not have about women in other professions, particularly my own. But I read all three Chicago papers every day. I care about what they say about law enforcement in this city. And I think you're a good police reporter.'

'Thank you.'

'That's why I was disappointed when your name came up in this case.'

Jennifer held her breath and slowly let it out as he continued.

'Truthfully, I was most disappointed when the top secret documents from John Lucas arrived at my home on Sunday, indicating the names of four officers who would be arrested in the Tuesday morning operation. My heart is always broken when I receive that kind of news.

'It comes in the form of a dossier containing all the essentials on the officer, his record, his years of service, everything. And it culminates in a careful listing — not detailed like it will be for the trial — but a listing of the offences which have necessitated the arrests.

'Yes, ma'am, I recognized that Officer Purcell was a man John had once considered for work with IAD. But you'd be amazed at how many men who are considered for that kind of work either don't want to do it or aren't qualified. We won't touch a man with *anything* on his record. If he had a tardiness problem when he first joined, it's a red flag.'

He paused for a long minute. Jennifer didn't know what to make of it. 'Are you saying that something in Jim's file disqualified him for IAD?'

'You see, Mrs. Grey, I wouldn't know

that. I gave permission for him to be considered, and more than a year later I read a file that contains a very damaging, very horrifying list of offences against society, against the department, against the law.'

'But it was a setup! He was working for Lucas!'

Commissioner Masek leaned forward and rested his chin on his fist, his elbow on the massive desk. He looked into her eyes with a blank expression. She could read nothing. He spoke slowly, carefully. 'You have a reason to want to believe that. The only reason I want to believe it is because it saddens me to think that even one patrol officer is involved in the kinds of things in which these four were involved. If for some reason that number could be reduced to three, it would soften the blow for me by just that much. But, Mrs. Grey, the idea of it is preposterous. I'm sorry to have to tell you that. I believe you are sincere; but I'm afraid your young friend is lying to you.'

Jennifer started to protest, but he raised a hand to silence her. 'Let me put it this way,' he tried again. 'Let's say I wanted to give you the benefit of the doubt. What could I do? I have no knowledge past what I told you. Yes, I find it ironic that a man who had a tremendous record, a man who was once considered for IAD, was eventually arrested by them. But that *is* the truth as I know it.

And unless someone in IAD tells me otherwise, I have to rely on the arrest documentation. And that looks extremely bad for Officer Purcell.'

Jennifer didn't want to cry. She wouldn't. How could this have happened? Was it possible Lucas thought his idea was so novel that he wanted *no one* else to know? Apparently, he had not considered this eventuality. But then no one had.

'Can you tell me anything from Chief Lucas's private file?'

'Yes, but I must first ask you to sign a statement that stipulates that you have been granted access to classified information and that if you ever disseminate it in any fashion, you can be prosecuted.'

His secretary dug out the form and brought it in. Jennifer signed quickly as Commissioner Masek scanned the typed list of the contents of Lucas's file. 'I'll read you only the pertinent items; I prefer not to show anything to you. The only thing I see here that could have any bearing on Officer Purcell is a list of appointments over the last year with individuals to whom he gives code names: Apollo, Cruiseship, Delta, Eagle.'

Jennifer pressed her fingers to her temples and stared at the floor. 'None of them mean anything to me,' she said sadly.

'They don't have to mean anything, and probably don't. When we use code names, we use them in categories, that's all. Sometimes it's birds — Robin, Dove, Sparrow, and all the rest. Sometimes it's characters from a classic. John was apparently using names from the space programme.'

'What if one of the names meant something to Jim?'

'Then we'd have only his word for it, wouldn't we?'

She nodded.

'Anyway,' he said, 'if I know John, he never would have told any of his contacts his code names for them.'

Jennifer stood and reached for Masek's hand. 'Thank you for seeing me at such short notice,' she said. 'Do I have any other recourse? Any at all?'

Masek covered her hand with both of his. 'Nothing I can think of,' he said. 'Unless John Lucas says your man was working for him, Purcell's in a lot of trouble.'

Jennifer stepped out of Masek's office just as his secretary was hanging up the phone. *God,* Jennifer prayed silently, *forgive my motive, forgive my selfishness, forgive anything I've done wrong in this whole mess. Just don't let Lucas die.*

His secretary pushed her intercom button. 'Mr. Masek?'

'Yes, Joan.'

'The hospital just called. Mrs. Lucas is asking for you.'

'*Mrs.* Lucas?'

'Yes, sir. She would like you to come right away, if possible.'

'What do I have this afternoon?'

'Sir, it was the doctor, and he said you should hurry.'

'Thanks, Joan. Cancel everything. Call the car.'

Masek flew out of his office, putting his coat on as he went. Jennifer had to run to keep up with him, a lump rising in her throat. *God, please!*

'Commissioner, may I go with you?'

As he waited for the lift, he appeared annoyed that she would even ask. He shrugged as if he really didn't know, couldn't decide, and wished she weren't there.

They descended in the lift together. He still hadn't said no, so she stayed with him. 'I won't get in the way.' He moved faster now, out the front door to his waiting car. 'I want to be there,' she said.

Suddenly he stopped and turned on her. 'Why?' he demanded angrily. 'Whatever for?'

'I don't know!' she said, almost shouting.

He climbed into the back seat and shut the door, leaving her standing there holding her coat, shivering and fighting tears. She was paralyzed, wondering if she should run around the building to her car and race to the hospital on her own. But she'd never get close to Lucas's room if she wasn't with the commissioner.

She clenched her fists and hung her head, then heard the commissioner's car stop at the corner and reverse. It screeched to a stop in front of her, and the back door flew open. She didn't hesitate.

When Masek and Jennifer stepped out of the lift in the intensive care unit, they saw the Lucas family standing in a waiting area at the end of the corridor, embracing each other and crying.

An emergency team was slowly leaving one of the rooms, and the commissioner and Jennifer knew. Lucas had died.

'No,' Masek moaned as he walked slowly toward the family. Jennifer's arms hung straight at her sides, and she forced herself to keep moving on her rubbery legs. Her breath came in short gasps.

Sylvia Lucas noticed Masek and fell into his arms, sobbing loudly and holding him tight. 'Oh, Joe, Joe,' she said. 'Thank you for coming!'

'I'm so sorry, Syl,' he said, his long arms wrapped around her.

'He was awake, Joe. He was awake when they called you. He talked.'

'He talked?'

'Yeah, Joe. Didn't make any sense, but he tried to talk to me.'

Jennifer stepped closer, her heart racing.

'That's nice, Syl,' Masek said. 'He was tryin' to say good-bye to you; you know that.'

'I don't know, Joe,' she said, trying to gain control of herself. 'He just said something crazy. It didn't make any sense to me. He said, "Thank the Eagle for me. Thank Purcell." What do you make of that?'

Masek turned in time to see Jennifer slump into a chair. She buried her face in her hands and sobbed. She and Masek had realized the bad news about John Lucas at the same instant. Now they both knew the goods news about Jim. It was over.